RANGE FEUD

RANGE FEUD

A WESTERN DUO

RAY HOGAN

THORNDIKE
CHIVERS

This Large Print edition is published by Thorndike Press, Waterville, Maine, USA and by AudioGO Ltd, Bath, England.
Thorndike Press, a part of Gale, Cengage Learning.

LIBRARY OF CONGRESS CATALOGING-IN-PUBLICATION DATA

Hogan, Ray, 1908–1998.
  Range feud : a western duo / by Ray Hogan.
    p. cm. — (Thorndike Press large print western)
  ISBN-13: 978-1-4104-3543-9 (hardcover)
  ISBN-10: 1-4104-3543-1 (hardcover)
  1. Large type books. I. Hogan, Ray, 1908–1998 Calaveras Hills.
  II. Title.
PS3558.O3473C35 2011
813'.54—dc22   2010049457

BRITISH LIBRARY CATALOGUING-IN-PUBLICATION DATA AVAILABLE

Published in 2011 in the U.S. by arrangement with Golden West Literary Agency.
Published in 2011 in the U.K. by arrangement with Golden West Literary Agency.

U.K. Hardcover: 978 1 445 83696 6 (Chivers Large Print)
U.K. Softcover: 978 1 445 83697 3 (Camden Large Print)

Printed in the United States of America
1 2 3 4 5 6 7 15 14 13 12 11

CONTENTS

■ ■ ■ ■

The Calaveras
Hills

■ ■ ■ ■

I

The land was the same. The hills had not changed nor had the high, depthless sky, so different from the smoky gray arch he had grown accustomed to during the war. The air was sharp, clean, and thin. That he noticed most of all. He had almost forgotten what it was like to breathe where the air was pure, not weighted down with the smell of gunpowder and sweat, or rotting flesh and charred timbers.

He pulled his wiry little buckskin to a halt, on the first low hill he reached after leaving the Canadian. Behind lay the long, flat plains to the east and south. Ahead were the rolling, grassy hills of his homeland and far beyond them rose the higher, black-chested mountains he once roamed. He took a deep and grateful breath. It was good to be back; after four long and bitter years of war it was wonderful to come home to peace and quiet — and the time when a man did not have to tread eternally on the alert, a gun ready in his hand.

Jeff Burkhart had been just eighteen when he rode out of the Calaveras country to answer Mr. Lincoln's call for men — more men. He had been received quickly and thereafter shuttled about haphazardly for several months, from post to post, before coming finally to permanent attachment with Sheridan at Perryville. He had remained with Fiery Phil from that day on, becoming one of the general's most trusted scouts for the duration of the war.

Now he was done with it; he was coming home. Back to his father, Tom, and the homestead along Seguro Creek, which was not a creek at all but a pretty fair-size stream, kept swift and deep by spring rains and winter snows. He was anxious to return, to begin working the dark, rich earth again, to put his hands to a plow and start growing and building things instead of destroying as he had been taught to do in the war years.

The Burkharts, father, mother, and son, had come West in the late 1850s. They had settled in the fertile Calaveras country — so recently opened by the government after General Kearney's bloodless conquest of once Mexican-held New Mexico Territory

— and begun a new life for themselves. It was as they had always hoped for: a land of good summers, of not too bitter and violent winters, where the air was always dry and clear and a man needed only to put seed in the ground to make a crop.

They did well. Tom Burkhart had a way with growing things and he was never a greedy man — never pressed the earth for too much. Sod was not broken unless there was a need, and he planted only what his family required to keep it comfortable and well. He knew the ways of Nature, realized that someday the cycle would change and the dry years and hard times would visit him as they did all men in the scheme of things.

And he had been right. For despite all his unique abilities with the earth, Tom Burkhart could not stay the hand of fate. Three years after they settled in the new territory, Jeff's mother sickened and died, victim of some malignant fever unknown to anyone. It had been a terrible blow to Tom Burkhart — took the keen edge off his love for the land. But the farm had continued to flourish.

A man like Tom Burkhart — that was the man that Tom's son, Jeff, hoped to be. Strong, able, respected — and having a way

with all things that grew. He had begun to follow in those footsteps when the war broke out. Once enlisted, he threw himself into the task of being a soldier just as he knew his father would have done, drawing upon his natural abilities and deep common sense. He became a good Army man — one of the best in his particular branch of the service — respected and relied upon by Sheridan.

In the closing months of the war, when the federal government had purchased several hundred of the latest model lever-action Henry rifles, Sheridan had personally obtained and presented one to his sergeant, Jeff Burkhart. It was a beautiful weapon, .44-caliber, sixteen shot, with the new type trouble free brass receiver.

In Jeff's expert hands it became a thing alive, a magic wand of destruction. He later cut its twenty-four-inch barrel to a brief eighteen, to improve his speed and ease in handling. So adept did he become with it that other members of his battalion soon began to refer to the pair as "Burkhart and Little Henry", and, by the time the war came to a close, they were well on the way to becoming a legend.

Now it hung in its well-oiled scabbard beneath him on the saddle. Never again

would it be necessary to draw the rifle against another man. Little Henry was a weapon of peace — something to be hung on pegs on the wall at home, to be used only on wolves and coyotes and such varmints. War and battles and dying men were behind it now.

Jeff touched the buckskin with his heels, started down the gentle slope. Not far ahead he could see the deeper colored purple of the ridge that lay beyond their homestead. Tom Burkhart had built his farm with that towering ledge to the north, utilizing it as a protection from the winds of winter that swept down periodically with icy breath.

Jeff felt his pulse quicken as he drew nearer and his glance began to take in more familiar landmarks and objects. There was Seguro Creek, running clear and wide, even so late in the summer. The snows apparently had been heavy in the mountains that past winter. He had killed a deer once, just beyond that wooded butte. And farther off to the left, there had been a bear.

Burkhart pulled the buckskin to an abrupt halt, a frown suddenly crossing his dark face. Smoke was rising from the valley below the purple ridge — far more smoke than an ordinary cooking fire would produce.

He sat quietly on the saddle, studying the lifting spirals — a young man yet, but fully grown in body and mind. He had wide shoulders on a slim frame and his dark hair was somewhat long, hanging well below the Army campaign hat he still wore — the last trace of a uniform once issued him. He had his father's wide mouth, his mother's calm, gray eyes, but the intentness — the keen readiness — about him was his own, initiated and developed by many hours and days and months of critical warfare.

The roll of smoke steadily thickened, began finally to boil. The white under surfaces of the clouds swept upward, whirled into a shifting mass, and turned to black.

Jeff Burkhart waited no longer. He urged the tired buckskin to a gallop, broke out at a fast pace across the long, sweeping valley that lay ahead. A bad fire of some sort was in progress at the homestead, either the house itself or some of the barns and lesser structures. It was no minor blaze, nor was it a grass fire. Jeff's eyes had looked upon too many burning towns and buildings to mistake the color of that smoke.

The buckskin crossed the valley, started up the opposite grade that led to the last crest from which he could look down onto the homestead. When he attained that point, he would be able to tell just what it was that burned.

He was halfway up the slope when he heard the first splatter of gunshots. The reports were quick, closely spaced. More like handguns than rifles. A sudden fear gripped him. Something was terribly wrong at the homestead; he was sure of that now. A huge fire — and now shooting. His father would be there alone. He had never been one to hire work done and such help, if actually needed, was seldom available in the Calaveras country. Tom Burkhart would be alone — and he was a man well up in his years now. He would be unable to put up much of a fight.

Burkhart pressed the faltering buckskin to his utmost, strained to reach the top of the slope. The shots still continued, a steady flow of distant-sounding, hollow *pops*. The horse began to tremble, to blow from his efforts. But they were near the top. Directly ahead the boiling smoke curled and leaped above the valley, shutting off a view of the purple ridge.

He was out of the saddle — rifle in hand — and on the ground before the buckskin made the last ten yards. He ran to the edge of the crest, threw his glance downward toward the scatter of structures that was his home.

A half a dozen riders wheeled in and out of the buildings, throwing their shots toward a small shed near the back of the yard. Beyond them, one of the barns — the largest structure where feed and various farm equipment were stored — roared and rumbled in a mass of seething flames.

The scene was a far cry from the peaceful, quiet landscape that Jeff had expected to find when he came wearily home.

II

Jeff wheeled quickly, was back on the saddle in half a dozen strides. He drove the heaving buckskin to the edge of the rise, then started him down the slope. He was still several hundred yards from the barnyard where the raiders circled, but he leveled his rifle, fired two fast shots.

They would fall short, he knew, but they might slow down the attack. And they would serve to let his father know help was on the way. He saw the cowboys glance toward the slope at the report of the Henry. They paused — but for only a moment and then continued their circling.

Burkhart fired another shot at the now

closer cowboys. He took more care this time, allowed for the distance. The bullet fell short again, dropped between the riders and the edge of the yard. They pulled into a group immediately, held a momentary conference. Jeff tried to watch them but he was having trouble staying on the saddle of the plunging buckskin. He held the rifle in one hand, reins in the other, while he leaned far back over the cantle to keep from being pitched forward.

Halfway down. Not much farther to the flats below. Then it would be just a short sprint to the yard of the homestead. His father was still holding out, still firing regularly from the tool shed in which he had taken refuge. He was shooting with the old Sharps carbine, the massive thunder of it booming over the lighter, more vicious sound of the pistols. There was someone else there, too. Jeff realized that as he drew nearer, someone with a lighter caliber gun.

He glanced ahead, sought to pick a route he might follow to the buildings, once he gained the foot of the slope. It would be mostly open ground, for little stray brush grew in the area that separated the hill from the homestead proper. To his left there was a thin stand of tamarack and dove weed. It did not offer protection but it was preferable to charging across an open field in the face of a half a dozen guns.

Three-quarters down. The shooting in the yard had lessened. Three of the riders had pulled off to one side, near the corral. They were firing at leisure and pointblank into the tool shed. Two more were near the house, not using their weapons at all, simply watching Jeff descend the slope. A sixth, a big man wearing a white hat, rode slowly toward the blazing barn, now almost consumed by flames and beginning to cave inward.

Jeff took a firmer grasp of his rifle. He would start using Little Henry the instant the buckskin regained his balance. The two riders who watched him evidently had it in mind to turn their guns on him as quickly as he was off the slope and became a practical target. They would never get that satisfaction, he decided grimly. A few quick and well-placed shots would turn them aside. He lifted the Henry and, with one hand, threw two bullets toward them.

Suddenly the buckskin was going down beneath him. He had only a fragment of time in which to kick his feet free of the stirrups. In the next instant he was hurtling through space, the buckskin churning up a boiling cloud of dust beneath him.

He struck the ground almost on all fours, went over in a long, headfirst dive. Lights flashed before his eyes as the rifle's barrel struck him but he did not lose consciousness. He went on over in a roll, sprawled out full length, no wind in his lungs. He could hear the two cowboys yelling, knew instinctively they were racing in for the kill.

He shook his head, sat up, momentarily dazed. He was aware he could not remain there on the ground — not for long. He got to his feet, shaky and not completely sure of what he was doing. He glanced around wondering about his horse. The buckskin, miraculously unharmed by the bad spill, stood ten feet behind him, the whites of his eyes showing bright, his brown coat well plastered with dust and other bits of trash.

Burkhart wheeled, ran for the horse. The two riders opened up at once. Bullets dug into the loose sand around Jeff's feet, droned by him with an uncomfortable nearness. He half turned, levered the Henry twice. The cowboys hauled up short, split apart.

He reached the nervous buckskin, vaulted into the saddle. He took another shot at the nearest rider as he spun about and dug for the tamarack. He thrust a hand into a side pocket of his jacket, brought out a half a

19

dozen or so cartridges, and, as the buckskin legged it for the breaks, he refilled the Henry's magazine to capacity. That done, he felt better. Now he could hold his own.

He reached the tamarack and dove weed without drawing more bullets from the two cowboys. He swung sharply right, down the brush, heading for the yard of the homestead. He broke out of the maze into a clearing just south of the buildings. He glanced over his shoulder, wondered what had become of the two riders sent to take care of him. Evidently they had lost sight of him when he cut into the brush. They were, at that moment, riding slowly toward it, watching it sharply for signs of his exact location.

He started to lay a shot or two at them, thought better of it. If their attention was drawn elsewhere for the next few minutes, it would afford him a chance to reach the yard, exchange shots with the other outlaws, or whatever they were, and perhaps allow him to gain the shed where his father and the person or persons with him were holed up.

He came into the open in time to see the man with the white hat, carrying a flaming brand from the ruined barn, ride up to its companion structure, a smaller building where livestock was generally quartered.

The cowboy tossed the burning length of wood through the open doorway, wheeled, and trotted his horse toward the center of the yard.

At that instant Jeff saw his father emerge from the tool shed, run in that faltering way of an old man toward the structure. The rider, who had been watching, immediately began to shoot, but Tom Burkhart reached the door unhurt, vanished inside.

Jeff drove for the small barn at a gallop. The man with the white hat halted, his gaze on the doorway into which Burkhart had disappeared. A moment later the homesteader appeared, carrying the torch. He ran into the open, threw the fiery brand well out into the yard where it could do no harm.

The white-hatted rider leveled his gun over the crook of his left arm. Jeff shouted, snapped a hasty shot at him but to no avail. Jeff saw the puff of smoke, heard the hollow *crack* of the pistol, and saw his father halt in mid-stride. He hung there for an instant, fell forward, then to his hands and knees. His hat dropped from his head, rolled off to one side in a loping, uneven way.

Wild with anger, Jeff aimed two more shots at the raider, saw him wheel sharply away as if just then aware of danger, and race for the company of the other cowboys.

They came together, swung out of the yard, all four now shooting as they rode. Jeff heard gunfire behind him. The other two must be coming in on him from the tamarack. He heard the *whine* of bullets overhead, instantly swerved to his left, placed a small juniper tree between them and himself. The tree was little more than a bush but it offered some protection since it masked his exact position for a brief time.

He rode out from the opposite end, his rifle up and ready. The two cowboys were coming in from the break at a hard run. He took good aim at the man slightly in the lead, squeezed the trigger. The cowboy jumped in the saddle, clutched at his arm.

Instantly he curved off to his right, his partner with him. As they raced along the edge of the tamarack, Jeff fired again, but the pair was going away fast and he missed the second shot. The other four men waited now at the foot of the slope off which he had just come. He saw the two join with them and all six immediately spin about and head south. Anger still a frenzied, driving force inside him, he rode forward after them a dozen yards, firing the Henry at will. But they were beyond effective range.

He turned then, rode quickly into the yard. His father lay full length, face down, silver hair shining dully in the streaming sunlight. A small, wiry man came from the tool shed, rifle in hand, and loped toward the still shape of Tom Burkhart.

They reached the fallen man almost at the identical moment. Jeff leaped from the saddle, dropped to his knees beside his parent. He took him by the shoulders, turned him over gently. Supporting him by one arm, he raised him off the ground a few inches. A broad, red stain covered Tom Burkhart's chest

"It bad?" the man who had sided the homesteader asked. He was thin and gaunt and as old, if not older than Tom Burkhart. He had a sharp, craggy face, eyes that were set too close, and thinning hair that was a faded brown.

Jeff nodded, cradling the frail body in his arms. "Got to get him inside. . . ."

"Murder! That's what that was!" the little man said in an explosion of words. "Tom was shot down in cold blood!"

Jeff stared at his father's features. Tom Burkhart had not changed much. A bit older, his hair somewhat whiter, but that same firm mouth and square, stubborn jaw.

"Them sneakin', bushwhackin' thieves!" the oldster continued, fairly beside himself with rage. "Day'll come when they'll be payin'! Count on that!"

Jeff got to his feet, lifting his light burden easily. He turned toward the house.

"Looks mighty bad," the little man said. "Reckon there ain't much use. But come on, I'll show you the way."

Grief and anger tearing at his soul, Jeff moved for the open doorway of the ranch house. "I know the way," he murmured.

III

Nothing had changed. As Jeff strode through the small square of parlor bearing the frail body of his father, he noted the same pictures were in their places upon the wall, the same braided, oval rugs were on the floor. The furniture was placed just as his mother had left it, even to the small rosewood butterfly table in the corner.

He reached the bedroom, entered, laid his parent upon the bed. He straightened up, seeing then that Tom Burkhart's eyes had opened at last, were staring up at him in a mixture of surprise and wonder.

Jeff said: "Hello, Pa. I'm home."

Tom Burkhart's gray lips parted in a weak smile of welcome. The man who had fought the raiders at his side moved in. He held a bottle of liquor and a glass in his hands. He

24

poured a stiff drink, held it to the home-steader's mouth while he gulped it down.

"Reckon that'll put a little starch in you, Tom," he said when Burkhart was finished. "This the boy you been tellin' me about?"

The homesteader nodded, reached his hand for Jeff's. "My son," he said in a slow voice. He shifted his eyes to the older man. "This here is Pete Langford, Jeff. Been workin' for me around the place, helpin' me some for a spell."

Jeff and Langford shook hands. The older man offered Jeff the bottle but he shook his head. "One of us ought to go for a doctor."

"Be startin' right now," Langford said, and turned away at once.

"No point," Tom Burkhart halted him. "Nothin' he could do for me. You both know that. Anyway, man's time comes, it comes. No doctor is goin' to change that."

Jeff knew his father was right. He had seen enough wounds during the war to know the mortal ones from the sort a man lived through. He pulled up a chair, the same rocker he had seen his mother sit in a thousand times or more, settled himself beside the bed.

He was at a loss for words; he did not know what to say to his father. Somehow the years had grown up between them, forming a towering barrier, leaving no common ground upon which they could meet. He had not wanted it that way. He had pictured his homecoming as different — a time when they could be together and talk about old times and work shoulder to shoulder in a world finally at peace. Instead he felt like a stranger — an unfortunate one who had walked in upon strife and death.

"Looks like you got home just in time," Tom Burkhart said with great effort. "That you comin' down off the east slope?"

Jeff said: "That was me. Heard the shooting and came fast as I could. Horse stumbled, else I'd have been here a bit sooner . . . maybe soon enough to prevent this."

Burkhart shook his head. "No, reckon it wouldn't have made no difference. Bound to happen. You're here now, that's what counts," He paused; his weary eyes searched Jeff's features closely. "You have a bad time of it in the war, Son?"

"No worse than any other man. I was with Phil Sheridan."

"Good officer, I hear tell. You get any wounds?"

"Nothing worth mentioning, Pa. I would have written only. . . ." Jeff faltered, trying to explain his failure to correspond during

26

the four years he was away.

"Never mind," Tom Burkhart said. "Know how it goes. Man's always on the move and writin' ain't ever very handy to get at. Besides, many a letter never got delivered."

Jeff shrugged. "Should have taken time to write anyway, Pa. Then maybe I'd have known you were having trouble and could have come home sooner. How long has this been going on?"

Pete Langford spoke up. "Most of a year, now."

Tom Burkhart seemed not to hear. "You home to stay?"

Jeff said: "From now on. Figure this is where I belong, where I want to be."

"That's good. Was sort of hopin' that was the way you'd feel about it. Lonesome around here, both you and your ma gone. Funny how things work out. You come back just when I'm leavin'."

"Pa, maybe a doctor could . . . ," Jeff fumbled, wishing now he had made Langford ride for help anyway.

Tom Burkhart wagged his head slowly. "We both know that'd be a waste of time. Don't fret yourself none about it. Just set where you are so's I can look at you. Your ma would have been proud of you, just like I am."

Pete Langford stepped up beside the bed, looked down at Burkhart. "They's a few chores I reckon I ought to be at, Tom. I'll be outside, doin' them."

The homesteader said: "Sure, Pete. And I'm mighty obliged to you for standin' by me. Appreciate it if you'll do the same for my boy here."

Langford extended his hand, shook Burkhart's gently. "You can figure on that, Tom. Long as he wants me." He wheeled, left the room.

"Gettin' a mite dark in here, Jeff," Burkhart murmured. "Them shades up?"

"They're up," Jeff replied. He looked more closely at his father, the tightness in his throat growing more pronounced. "There anything you want? Another drink?"

"No," Tom Burkhart said, "no need for that, either. Just keep settin' there, like I asked you to. Your ma will be wantin' to know about you, and when I see her and. . . ."

The words halted. Jeff waited for them to continue. When they did not, he rose, laid his head against his father's breast. He straightened up after a moment, his face stiff and solemn. Tom Burkhart was dead.

For a long time he stood there, looking down into the pinched, now quiet face. All

28

thoughts of the future, of the peaceful way of life he had envisioned so many times, receded slowly in his mind. A cold, bitter hatred seeped in, quickly filled their place. He reached down, drew a thin coverlet over his father's lifeless body, turned to the door. He walked into the parlor where Pete Langford waited.

"It over?" the old man asked, rising to his feet.

Jeff nodded. "What's this all about, Pete? What's been going on around here?"

Langford walked to the door, opened it, spat a brown stream of tobacco juice into the yard. "Trouble . . . plenty of it. This is the third time they hit your pa's place."

"Why? What did they have against him? He never did a living man any harm."

"Reckon that's gospel but that ain't what it's all about. They been tryin' to drive him offen this place same as they've drove off every other homesteader in this country."

"They? Who are they?"

"Why, cattle raisers! Ranchers! This valley is mighty fine grazing for beef. They want it all . . . bad . . . and they sure just about got it now."

Jeff Burkhart thought for a long minute. "Maybe, but not all of it, not yet. They'll have to kill me, too."

Pete Langford nodded his vigorous approval. "Sort of figured you'd be that way. Just like your pa."

"My father built this place with his own two hands. Sweated over every square inch of it. He and my mother . . . and me. Nobody is going to take it away from us."

"That sure sounds fine," Langford said, "but the odds is a mite bad. You any idea what you're up against?"

"Been times in my life before when the odds weren't so good. Guess I can keep on bucking them right here." Jeff stopped, picked up his rifle from the table where Langford had laid it. "Who was that man with the white hat? He'll be where I start."

"The one who shot down your pa? That'd be Carl Animas."

"Carl Animas?"

"A bad one. Tough gunslinger. Sort of heads up that hardcase bunch you saw with him."

"Where will I find him?"

Langford scratched at the bridge of his long, bony nose. "Headed south when they left here. Reckon they lit out for town."

"Town? What town?" There had been no such place four years ago.

Langford stared at him for a time. "Why, Riflestock, of course. Couple hours easy ride, due south."

Jeff swung toward the doorway. He halted, his hand on the latch. "Appreciate it if you'll look after things. Fix up a coffin. . . ."

"Sure. Some boards in the shed. I'll nail up one right away. You want to put him back there on the hill, next to your ma, I take it."

Jeff said: "Yes, but hold up on that part. I want to be here. Should make it back by dark."

Langford squinted at him. "Just be sure you do make it, son. That Carl is a slick one. Got everybody in this country buffaloed."

Jeff nodded. "I'll be back."

IV

Riflestock. Jeff Burkhart pulled to a halt at the edge of town and stared. Where, four years or so ago, there had been only the sprawled, slanted roof building of Hinton's General Store, there now were more than a dozen other business houses. They ran out from either corner of Hinton's in square, false-fronted shapes — even faced it from the opposite side of the dusty street. There was a hotel, a café, three or four saloons, a barbershop, livery stable, saddlery — just about anything a man could look for includ-

31

ing a town marshal.

Jeff, astride a jet-colored gelding, in deference to the worn buckskin he had ridden back home on, started down the street at a slow walk. He had paid little attention to the horse Carl Animas had been riding, or to any of those who had accompanied the outlaw. It was going to be a matter of search. Most likely he would find the gunman in one of the saloons.

He drew in before Hinton's, that structure marking the center of town, more or less, and dismounted. With his rifle crooked in his arm, he tied the black to the post and moved up onto the wide gallery fronting the broad store building.

At that moment the screen door opened and a girl emerged. Jeff, his thoughts placed solely on Carl Animas, wheeled quickly, automatically, and faced her. She gave him a startled glance, halted suddenly.

Jeff allowed the Henry to lower immediately. The girl stared at him with interest. She was slight, well-shaped, her hair a bright red. She had, Jeff thought, the greenest eyes he had ever seen, and at that moment the angriest.

"Sorry, ma'am," he murmured. "You sure startled me some."

She looked him over carefully. "You always

that jumpy with a gun?"

"Only sometimes," he replied quietly. He glanced off down the street. Two men had come through the swinging doors of a saloon, appropriately named the Moonshiner. They walked toward several horses tethered to the long rail in front of it. Neither of them wore a white hat. He felt her eyes still upon him, frankly curious and wondering.

"You're new here, aren't you?"

He said: "Manner of speaking, I am. Lived here before the war."

"Oh, I see. You've just returned."

"Yes, ma'am, just this day."

"Don't say ma'am to me!" she exclaimed impatiently. "I'm not that old! Not even as old as you!"

The batwings of the Moonshiner flung open again. Three more cowboys came onto its gallery. The one in the center, a short stocky man with a broad dark face, glanced down the street. He wore a wide-brimmed white hat, pushed at the moment to the back of his head.

"No, ma'am," Jeff Burkhart said softly, absently, and moved off Hinton's porch into the ankle-deep dust of the lane.

With the rifle in his right hand, hanging muzzle down at his side, he walked slowly for the three riders. They were yet in the shade of the saloon, talking among themselves. The man in the white hat leaned with his back against a supporting pillar of the porch roof. The two others faced him. Burkhart trod at deliberate pace toward them until he was no more than a dozen yards away. There he halted, his eyes on the trio.

"One of you Carl Animas?"

At his question they straightened, turned to face him. For a long minute they looked him over. The one in the white hat finally spoke.

"That's me. What's on your mind?"

"You."

The gunman's expression did not change. "Who are you, mister?"

"Name's Burkhart. That was my pa you shot down back there."

One of the others nodded his head. "Thought I knew that jasper. He was the bird that come roarin' off the hill."

"Another Burkhart," Animas murmured.

The two men flanking the gunman drifted slowly off to either side. Jeff was conscious of others along the street then, men and women, curious and attracted by the words that had been spoken. He did not look away, kept his attention on the gunslinger.

Animas stepped off the gallery, walked with utmost care into the center of the street.

"So?"

"Figured maybe you'd like to try and finish up the job. I'm the last of the family," Jeff said.

Animas's eyes were small, empty pockets beneath their shelf of heavy brows. He had pushed his hat forward now. It shaded his face from the hard sunlight.

"Reckon a man ought to do a job up right, sure enough," he said. "Don't see no iron on your hip. You goin' to jaw me to death, that it?"

Someone near the saloon laughed. Farther along in the town a dog barked.

"I'll use this," Jeff replied, moving the short-barreled Henry slightly.

"That rifle? Boy, I hate to take advantage, but you ain't got a prayer with that thing. I'll have three bullets in your belly before you can get it to your shoulder."

"I'll take my chances. How about your friends there?"

"I kill my own snakes," Animas said. "They'll mind their own knittin'."

Burkhart nodded. "Better for them if they do."

Animas laughed. "You hear that, boys? He

35

sure is a cool one. I see now why the old man was so hard to convince."

Jeff watched the gunman through eyes pulled down to shut out the glare. The street was quiet, deserted now, but a half a hundred persons were looking on from the safety of stores and other buildings. He took a firm grasp of Little Henry, allowed his thumb to rest on the curved, ribbed top of the hammer. This would be a test of speed, of accuracy. And there would be no second chance. Animas, a gunman, apparently of wide repute, would be deadly. He would have to handle his weapon with greater efficiency than he had ever before shown.

He felt tension begin to build along his spine, pluck at his nerves. In the breathless hush he said: "Any time you're ready, killer."

The smirk faded from Carl Animas's features. His face now was a stolid mask, completely lifeless. His colorless eyes seemed to have receded ever farther into their dark sockets. Jeff watched the man narrowly, waited for that first, small break that would be the signal.

It came almost immediately, the slightest twitch of the gunman's lips. Jeff brought his weapon up with a snap of his wrist, finger tight on the trigger, in the swift, fluid manner he had perfected during the war. He released his thumb as the Henry lined on its target. The rifle bucked in his hand. Animas, his pistol out and rising, paused in motion. He pulled himself to his toes. A frown distorted his face. The barrel of his pistol tipped downward, and the man started to fall.

At that instant Jeff saw movement on the gallery of the saloon. He threw himself to one side, levered his rifle with a quick flip of his hand. He heard the *crash* of a pistol held by one of the two cowboys who had been with Animas — just which one he was not sure. He fired at the puff of smoke, went headlong to the dusty street. He rolled, levered the Henry again, snapped a second shot at the other man now trying to draw his own weapon. The cowboy wheeled, ducked for cover inside the saloon.

Burkhart waited a long minute, then got to his feet. Eyes on the saloon's swinging doors, he advanced toward them slowly. He reached the porch, stepped up onto it, moved the batwings. Rifle poised and ready in one hand, he pushed back one side with the other. A half dozen men faced him, their expressions blank. The bartender ceased his polishing of the bar top.

"Your man just went out the back way, mister," he said.

Burkhart's glance shifted from him to the others ranged along the counter. "Anybody got a mind to take up where he left off?"

One or two shook their heads. Others simply turned around, placed their attention upon the glass that was before them. Jeff stepped back, allowed the door to swing shut. He pivoted on his heel to the street. Several men had gathered around Carl Animas. No one had yet ventured up onto the porch where the other cowboy lay.

Burkhart walked to the sprawled figure. One glance told the man was dead; the bullet had caught him squarely in the chest, close to the heart. He continued on, came off the gallery, tension still holding him tight. He strode to the center of the street, let his gaze cover the few persons clustered about Carl Animas.

"One of you the marshal?"

Several shook their heads. Another man, a short, heavy individual with a gold watch chain swung across his paunch, spoke up.

"Wade's out of town. So's Vic Antrum, his deputy."

Jeff said: "When they get back, tell them about this. And tell it right. It was a fair fight. You all saw that. They want to ask any questions, they'll find me at my place . . . Burkhart's."

"You Tom's boy?"

"I am."

"I hear you say Carl killed your pa?"

"You did. Shot him down while he and five others raided the place, set fire to one of the barns. I got there too late to stop it, but I mean to finish it. I don't know what's going on in this country, but you can tell the marshal I'm finding out."

"Well, maybe you just better find out first before you go talkin' so high and wide," a cowboy standing directly across from Jeff advised.

Burkhart leveled his gaze upon him. "You run with Animas and his bunch?"

"Not me," the man said quickly. "Just sort of figured you ought to know you was bitin' off a mighty big hunk to chew on."

"Maybe," Jeff said, "but if there's somebody around here looking to start a war, I'm ready to accommodate them. Just rode in from four years of fighting and killing. Reckon I'm willing to carry it on for another four if that's what it takes."

"Nobody's wanting a war . . . ," a voice murmured.

"Then what's this talk of driving the homesteaders out of this country? Today I got a pretty fair sample of how they mean to do it."

"We don't want no war, not here in town, anyway," a man with a dirty white apron draped across the front of his bulging stomach said. "It's something between the cattlemen and the squa− . . . settlers. We don't want it here in Riflestock."

Jeff Burkhart let his cool, gray eyes run over the man with deliberate scorn. He shrugged. "I'd say you got it, friend, right here today," he said, and, turning, walked back to where his horse awaited him.

V

It was not yet dark when he rode into the yard of his father's place — *his* place, now, he realized with a start. Pete Langford was standing in the doorway of the main house. He came out into the open, placed a questioning look at Jeff. He apparently saw the answer in the set of the younger man's jaw and in his eyes. He nodded, took the reins of the black, and led him off to the barn.

Jeff entered the house, turned into the bedroom. Langford had completed his job. All that remained of Tom Burkhart was in a blanket-lined wooden box. Jeff stood quietly for a moment, studying his father's stilled features. He wished there was some way to tell him Carl Animas was dead, that he had served warning he would fight to the end to keep the Burkhart holdings in the Calaveras country. But there was no way of doing that now. He could only hope his father knew — somehow understood.

He picked up the lid of the coffin and, with the hammer and nails Langford had left on the table, fastened it securely in place. Before he had completed his task, Pete Langford was back, standing off to one side in silence.

Finished, they carried the box to the low hill back of the buildings. Langford had already dug the grave, and, with two ropes, they lowered the casket into it.

Langford uncovered his head. He glanced at Jeff's taut face, cleared his throat.

"The Lord giveth and the Lord taketh away. Seems to me like You tooketh Tom Burkhart mighty early, Lord. He was a good man. Don't reckon I ever met a better one. But I suspect You know what You're doin', Lord. Amen."

"Amen," Jeff echoed quietly.

"You go on ahead, boy. I'll finish this up," Langford said after that.

Jeff shook his head. "I'll help," he said, and reached for the long-handled scoop.

Together they completed the burial, and, when the mound was smoothed off to match that of his mother's grave, lying close by, Pete Langford handed him a marker. It bore only the name: Tom Burkhart.

"Didn't know the date," the older man explained, "leastwise when your pa was born. Up to you to furnish that part."

"Can't say as I know for certain," Jeff replied. "Have to look it up in the family Bible. Do that tonight and tomorrow I'll letter it on."

"Good," Langford said, gathering up the tools. "Thing like that ought to be right. I'll go on ahead, stir up a bite of supper. You come eat when you're ready."

He did not wait to hear any reply from Jeff but moved off into the steadily falling darkness. Jeff remained still, his mind at rest, and he reached back through the years. He was remembering the time when his mother was alive, when his father had moved about in their small world like a never-faltering giant, capable of all things. There had been no man equal to his pa; he could accomplish anything, as if he had the touch of magic.

It had been a wonderful life, and a happy one. Jeff Burkhart regretted now that he had gone — had been away the four years his father had likely needed him most. The death of Jeff's mother had made a lonely

42

man of Tom Burkhart, but Jeff, in his hurry to get into the war, had given that no consideration. He had actually compounded the problem by leaving, by considering only himself and his own personal desires.

His father had not tried to stay him. He had merely agreed with the arguments that it was something that Jeff should do. And Jeff had ridden away with Tom Burkhart's blessing, cautioned only to take care of himself and be a man at all times. Now he was back — but too late, too late for them all. He would not let it end there, he told himself in the darkness of the little hill. The happiness and joy the Burkharts had brought to the valley might end for them in the cold enclosure of the grave — but the memory of it would never vanish. Not so long as he lived.

He returned to the house soon after that. He found Pete Langford waiting and together they sat down to the square-shaped kitchen table. They ate in silence. When they were finished, they moved into the parlor.

Langford produced a well-scorched pipe and Jeff, digging around his person until he found the makings, rolled himself a cigarette.

The brier at last going, Langford voiced his question: "What happened in town?"

"Met up with Animas in the street. I shot him before he shot me."

Langford's scraggly eyebrows lifted sharply. "Reckon you must be mighty handy with that sawed off rifle of yours. You come up against anybody else?"

"Two men with him. One of them cut and run. The other one tried to pot-shoot me, but I got there first. Tall, thin man. Had a scar on his chin."

Langford thought for a moment. "That'd be Charlie Searles. Another one of Ben Sutter's hired killers."

Jeff glanced up. "Whose?"

"Ben Sutter. He's the rancher that's back of all this. Got hisself a two hundred thousand acre spread to the north and still wants more."

"Animas and the others work for him, is that it?"

"Sure. 'Course, he's laid up. Got throwed by a horse and has to stay in bed most of the time. But he calls the shots, just the same. Got a foreman name of Riley Claybourne that does his gettin' around for him."

"Don't recall any of those names," Burkhart mused. "Must have moved into the country after I left."

"Been around four, maybe five years now.

Only it wasn't till after beef prices got high that Sutter started his spreadin' out." Pete Langford stopped. His eyes filled with a deep bitterness. "Drove me off my place about two years back."

Jeff waited a few minutes, his gaze on the old man's hate-withered features. "Animas in on it, too?"

"Nope, 'twas another bunch of hired killers then. They come and they go. Reckon Carl and Searles is the first to leave feet foremost, howsomever. Makes no difference about who did the work. Sutter was behind it."

"Claybourne with him long?"

"Sure. He's been around ever since Ben Sutter hit this country. Does just what Ben tells him, and then maybe adds a little extra of his own. Handles them gunnies he hires like a 'skinner handles mules. Sort of a nice-lookin' feller but meaner'n salted bear underneath."

Jeff said: "Where was your place?"

" 'Bout ten miles northeast of here. Place they called Yankee Meadows. Not much of a spread but I was gettin' started. Then Sutter sent his bunch in, shot up my herd, burned down my house."

"You were raising cattle? Thought you were homesteading, like my pa."

Langford nodded his head. "Did start out that way. Had it in mind first to farm, then I saw there was goin' to be some money made in cattle, so I got me a little herd together and started."

"And Ben Sutter drove you out. You lose everything?"

"Mighty nigh! Oh, he sent Claybourne over with some money, enough to pay for my herd and what he'd been offerin' me for my land. Said he was sorry about the boys killin' the stock. All a big mistake, he said."

"You settle with him?"

"Sure. Wasn't nothin' else to do. I took his money, signed over the deed, and walked off. Could see they was no use buckin' Ben Sutter. But I'd 'a' like to have stayed! I'd 'a' like to have had it out with Ben Sutter and showed him he wasn't near as big shucks as he thinks! And someday somebody's goin' to do just that. Sure hope I'm around to see old Ben crawlin' in the dirt!"

Langford's face was flushed, his eyes bright. Jeff waited until he had calmed a bit. Then: "He the only one around here with the grabs?"

"Only one. Some more ranchers farther north and west. Hear they're doin' the same thing. Guess the day for homesteadin' is done with. Goin' to be cattle country."

"Doesn't anybody put up a fight?"

"Against hired guns? Not much! And they wasn't nothin' the marshal could do, either. Everything was all legal when it was over with."

"Nothing legal about murder and burning property," Jeff said dryly.

Langford wagged his head. "That's for certain. I figure somebody slipped up there. Don't think your pa was supposed to get killed . . . leastwise, not that way."

"Meaning what?"

"Well, Tom had been buckin' them for quite a spell. I figure they decided it was about time for him to have an accident or somethin'. If I was to be doin' some guessin', I'd say they figured to throw him into that barn, after he was shot. Then folks around here'd think he got himself burned to death. Couldn't nobody prove how the fire got started, and just put it all down as an accident. But you showed up and that changed things a mite."

"But you were here. You saw what happened."

"Sure, and I reckon the only reason I'm still alive and kickin' is because you rode in. Likely I'd've been right there inside that barn with your pa. Carl Animas wouldn't have left no witnesses."

47

Jeff Burkhart made no reply. He rolled himself another cigarette, fired a match with his thumbnail. He blew out the small, yellow flame, tossed the stick into the cold fireplace.

"What you figure to do, Jeff?" Langford asked. "Sell out or stay and fight?"

"This was my father's place. He'd want me to stay on it. And that's what I'll do. How many gunmen has Sutter got on his payroll?"

"Half a dozen or so around all the time. They don't do no cattle work, just handle the rough stuff that has to be done. You takin' care of Carl and Searles will short hand him a bit but he's still got Abilene Dow and four, five others. And he can always hire more."

Jeff said: "Right. And a man can keep shooting them down and never run out. Thing to do is to go right to the head of the problem."

"Sutter hisself?"

"Sutter himself. Comes tomorrow morning, I'm riding over there and tell him to call off his wolves. If he won't listen, then he's in for a dose of his own medicine."

"Good! Good!" Langford said, his yellowed teeth exposed in a broad grin. "Figured you wouldn't be takin' none of him layin' down! You want I should go along?"

"You best stay here," Jeff answered. "Somebody ought to keep an eye on the place. Fort up in one of those sheds where you can hold out in case they hit us again. I won't be gone long."

Langford grunted his satisfaction and approval. "I can hold out myself but you better be mighty careful around Ben Sutter. Be walkin' right into a nest of rattlers. That whole danged bunch will be gunnin' for you after what happened to Carl and Searles."

"That'll make it even," Burkhart said coolly. "I'll be gunning for them."

VI

From the crown of a low hill Jeff Burkhart studied Ben Sutter's B-Bar-S Ranch. It was a fine spread, one any man would like to own. Trees had been planted about the place for shade and the yard was well kept. Besides the long, low ranch house there were numerous barns, sheds, and corrals as well as comfortable-looking quarters for the crew. All were set in a grassy hollow where a small, brightly running stream cut a silver path across its width. The vast acreage where Sutter's herds grazed was flung out on all sides, extending to boundaries not clearly defined in any man's mind.

Jeff watched three riders lope in the yard, pull up before the rail fronting the larger of the two bunkhouses. They dismounted, two of the men heading into their quarters while the third crossed the open area and entered the main house by a side entrance. That would be the kitchen, Jeff concluded, noting the chimney and the collection of garbage and trash cans standing just outside the door.

The front of the ranch house could be reached without riding into the yard, he noted. That simplified matters, since it would not be necessary to cross over in view of the bunk quarters. He was not forgetting Pete Langford's words of caution; he would find no friends on Sutter's ranch.

If he could make Ben Sutter understand that further persecution on the part of his men would mean bloodshed for both sides, since he was determined not to sit by as did the other homesteaders and allow himself and his place to be overrun, then he would have accomplished something. Perhaps, by so doing, he could halt the smoldering war in the Calaveras Hills before it burst into a full-scale blaze.

Sutter was the key figure; he could halt

matters where they presently stood, or he could permit it to run on until an explosion resulted. At any rate — and risk — Jeff Burkhart felt the rancher should be given the opportunity for making his choice and decision. Since the shootings in Riflestock, Sutter would know he no longer dealt with helpless, fearful farmers, unable and unwilling to fight back. That could make a difference in his thinking.

He nudged the buckskin into motion and started down the gentle slope. He slanted for the rail at the front of the house, intentionally avoiding the yard — not in the sense that he was ducking trouble, but with the thought that he was on a peaceful mission. He was there to talk, not to fight. That, if it proved out so, would come later.

It was not to be that way.

He reached the foot of the hill, started across the level ground for Sutter's main house. The bunkhouse door flung back. Three men walked into the yard, cut to their right, pursuing a course that would intercept his line of progression before he reached the low-roofed structure. He realized they probably had been watching him from the building's windows for some time.

He gave no outward indication that he had noticed them but continued on at an even, unchanged pace. But his hand tightened about the Henry rifle lying across his knees; his thumb moved up, hooked over the hammer, his forefinger increased its pressure on the trigger. If there was to be a showdown right in Ben Sutter's yard, he was ready.

They reached the hitch rail ahead of him, halted just beyond it, three dark-faced men with restless, quick eyes and low-hung guns. Jeff kneed the buckskin up to the bar, halted, never for an instant taking his own glance from the trio of hardcases. He sat for a long time, staring at them, as if assessing the possibilities, and then deliberately swung down.

"Who you lookin' for?" the man in the center of the group demanded in a threatening voice. He was a thin, dangerous-looking man with straw for hair and empty blue eyes. Somehow, he seemed familiar to Burkhart.

Jeff draped the leathers over the rail. "Not for you, mister."

"Maybe you're goin' to get me anyway," the gunman replied. "You got a hell of a lot of crust, ridin' in here."

"Why? A man can walk through a nest of snakes, if he's careful."

The rider to the left of the blond stirred angrily. "What're we supposed to do,

52

Abilene? Just stand here? They's three of us. . . ."

Jeff let his gaze come to a full stop on the man speaking. The corners of his mouth pulled down into a harsh grin. He lifted the Henry rifle suggestively, allowed it to settle back at his side. "And there's ten big slugs in his gun. They make a mighty nasty hole in a man. You start something, I'll get two of you before I go down, the third man then."

The blond said nothing. Jeff recognized him at that moment; he was the third man that had been with Carl Animas, the one who had fled through the saloon. He flung a look of contempt at the man. Abilene, one of the others had called him. Abilene Dow. Langford had mentioned the name.

"I'm going inside and talk to Ben Sutter. You got any notions about stopping me, mention them right now."

Burkhart walked slowly around the rail, crossed before the three men. Less than ten feet separated him from them. He moved with deliberate care. He had no illusions about emerging from a clash with them unhurt; three against one at such quarters were rough odds. But he had them at a disadvantage. The cocksure boldness he was displaying had knocked them off balance, left them unsure. And to that was added the experience Abilene Dow had undergone the previous day in Riflestock.

"Somebody go get Riley," Dow murmured. "See if you can find him, Chick. Denver and me will wait here."

Burkhart reached the short, board sidewalk that led up to the front of Sutter's house. The gunmen were to his side now and slightly to the rear. He continued on toward the gallery, boot heels rapping solidly and with slow precision on the unpainted wood. He gained the porch, crossed it, and knocked on the door. He wheeled around slowly. Some of the tension drained from his tall frame as he again faced the gunmen. Walking away from them had presented several tight moments; his back had offered to them a most inviting target.

He rapped again on the door. Almost immediately it opened. He stared at the girl who stood before him. It was the redhead with the green eyes he had seen at Hinton's store.

She looked at him in startled surprise for a brief time. Then recovering, she said: "Yes?" Her voice was cool, with no friendliness in it.

"I want to talk to Ben Sutter."

The girl shook her head. She was wearing

some sort of light, cotton dress that fit her figure snugly and was of a pale lavender shade that set off the color of her hair. She said: "I'm Ben Sutter's daughter. What do you want to talk to him about?"

It was Burkhart's turn to be surprised. He cast a glance over his shoulder at Dow and the other cowboy, came back to her. "Mind if I step inside?" he asked, and pushed on by her into the room. "Get a ticklish feeling in the back of my neck when I know there's a couple of gunslicks behind me."

Ben Sutter's daughter was suddenly angry. Her eyes snapped and her checks burned brightly. "What do you want here? You going to shoot down my father, too, like you did those two men in town yesterday?"

"They had their chance," Burkhart replied, his voice going cold.

"You deliberately picked a quarrel with them! I saw that, I saw you do it! You forced them to fight you."

He nodded. "Yes, ma'am, that's right. And the reason I did, in case you don't know, is that one of them, Carl Animas, had just murdered my father."

The effect of his words was no less forceful than a blow from his hand. She stared at him. "No . . . I don't believe that."

He shrugged. "Maybe you should have

stuck around town a bit longer, heard all the story. It and a few other things."

"Those two men . . . they worked for us. They were B-Bar-S riders."

"That's right, Miss Sutter. Animas and five more of your crew hit my father's place yesterday afternoon. They burned down our barn, tried to set fire to another one where we kept our livestock. My father attempted to stop them and Carl Animas killed him in cold blood. I got there just as it all happened but too late to stop it. I followed Animas into town and settled with him. Your other man, Searles his name was, horned in and got the worst of it."

Her face had become quiet. She stepped back, a steadily rising fear beginning to show in her eyes. "And now you've come to kill my father. I won't let. . . ." She stopped talking, darted for the door to summon the men from the outside.

He was before her in a single stride, blocked her way. "No. I'm not here to kill anybody. I'm hoping that's done with now. I'm here to talk, nothing else. I want no more trouble and I'm willing to call it quits where it stands if your father will listen to reason and do the same."

She stared up into his face, not yet fully convinced of his intentions. Her glance dropped to the rifle in his hand. "Will you leave that gun in here if I take you to him?"

Jeff Burkhart shook his head. "Sorry, ma'am, that's something I can't do, not around here. Where I go, it goes." He watched her face cloud with suspicion. "Not that I don't trust you or maybe even your father. I just don't trust the men you've got working for you."

She bit at her lower lip, moved back into the center of the room.

"You have my word. I mean no harm to you or your father," he said, understanding her indecision. "I'm here to talk, that's all. If there's any trouble, it will come after I leave."

"All right," she said then, "I'll take your word, Mister . . . ?"

"Jeff Burkhart."

"Mister Burkhart. My father is an invalid. I suppose you know that. He may be asleep. Follow me."

She turned, left the room, motioning for him to come, also. They passed down a short hallway, stopped before a closed door. The girl opened it, glanced inside. He looked over her shoulder to the slight figure lying with closed eyes on a bed.

She shut the door, faced Jeff. "I'm sorry. He's sleeping."

Burkhart did not move. "This is pretty important, to him as well as me. Maybe you ought to wake him up."

She shook her head. "I can't," she said, and pushed by him. "Come back into the parlor. I'll explain why."

VII

Once again in the front room of the ranch house, Jeff Burkhart stepped first to the window, glanced out. Dow and the other man still stood near the rail. The third man had not returned. He felt the girl at his shoulder.

"You took a chance coming here, didn't you?"

"Be worth it," he replied, "if I can get this ironed out with your father. What's the name of the man out there with Dow?"

She looked through the window a second time. "I don't know. I don't know either of them."

"You don't know?" Burkhart echoed. "They work for you, don't they?"

"Of course," she said, turning away, "but I don't have anything to do with the crew. Riley Claybourne, our foreman, handles that, and has ever since Father got hurt."

"Your father . . . you were going to explain

why we couldn't wake him up."

She crossed the room slowly, halted near a table. Sunlight, stealing in from another window, glinted against her hair, caused it to glow with a brighter intensity.

"He hasn't been out of this house since he was hurt. He spends his time either in that bed or, if he feels up to it, sitting in a chair. Most of the time he is in pain, unable to find rest at all. When that happens, I have to give him laudanum, so he can sleep. That's why I can't awaken him now."

Burkhart said: "I see. I'm sorry about it."

"Can't you come back later? Tomorrow morning, perhaps."

"Doubt if I'll get a second chance," he said with a wry grin.

"Then tell me what you have to say. I'll repeat it to him when he's awake."

Burkhart considered her suggestion for a moment, decided it was the only, if not the best, way to handle the problem. Immediately he went into the details of the brewing range war and what it would eventually amount to. He made his plea for peace to her, just as he had intended to make it to Ben Sutter, and gave her also his promise of a hard and bitter war, with no quarter given, if B-Bar-S riders continued their depredations. When he was finished, the girl turned,

59

walked again to the window.

"I don't believe my father is aware of this," she said. "Maybe that sounds like an excuse. But you don't know my father. He is a kind and just man. We need more grazing land, yes. Most cattle ranchers do, but he is willing to buy it and pay a fair price when he does. That is just what he has done in the past. I know because there are a few deals I have known about."

"But if a man won't sell out to him, do you know what happens then? Do you know about the raids your riders make to force a man to terms?"

She shook her head. "No, and I don't think my father does, either. He doesn't do business on that kind of a basis."

"But he does," Burkhart reminded her softly. "I brought you proof of that."

She came around slowly, met his gaze. "I'll tell my father all you've said, Mister Burkhart. Now, I'll ask a promise of you . . . that you won't do anything, that there won't be any more killing until I have had a chance to tell him all the things you've told me. Will you give me your promise?"

Burkhart said: "For my part, you have it. I can wait a day if you say so. What about your own crew? Will they be bound by the same promise?"

"They will. I'll tell Claybourne."

"Good. When can I expect to hear from you?"

"By noon tomorrow. And you needn't come here. I'll ride over to your place."

Burkhart said — "Obliged." — and started to wheel about. At that moment the door flung open. A tall, well-built man stepped into the room, his face flushed and angry.

Burkhart's reflexes were automatic. The rifle came up in a swift arc. The muzzle centered on the man's breast, steady and promising.

The girl's voice broke the sudden silence. "It's still customary to knock when you enter this house, Riley," she said in a sharp voice. "Lower your gun, Mister Burkhart. This is Riley Claybourne, our foreman."

Jeff allowed the weapon in his hand to relax. He nodded to Claybourne, a good-looking, dark man with an air of cold-steel authority about him. Claybourne did not offer to shake hands and Burkhart made no overture.

"What's he doing here, Cam?"

The girl stiffened perceptibly at the question. "He came on business. To see Father," she replied after a moment.

"Expect I can guess why," Claybourne said, switching his dark eyes to Burkhart.

61

"Murder is a pretty good reason," Jeff said, not liking the man at all.

"Murder? Any man has the right to defend himself."

"You speaking of Carl Animas or of my father?"

"Both," Claybourne said coolly. "Animas had a right to protect himself from your father. If your father got the worst of it, you can't blame anyone else."

Jeff Burkhart stared at Claybourne. "Is that what you believe? Did somebody tell you that?"

"I stand by my men," the foreman said. "I've no reason not to."

"You've got reason aplenty now!" Jeff exclaimed. "It was murder, nothing less, when Animas shot down my father. I know. I was there and saw it happen."

Claybourne shrugged his shoulders. "I'd expect you to say that, of course." He turned to the girl. "Cam, there's no sense in you taking it on yourself to listen to people like this man. There will be a lot of them coming by now. Send them on to me. Let me handle them."

"Just what you'd like!" Burkhart broke in. "Keep Ben Sutter in the dark about what goes on. . . ."

"I'm paid to run this ranch," Claybourne

said. "I'll do it the best way I know how."

"And with hired guns."

"If necessary. A ranch as big as B-Bar-S naturally makes enemies. It's part of my job to maintain protection."

Jeff Burkhart took a long step forward, thrust his face close to Claybourne's. "You send one more raiding party to my place, mister, and you'll need protection for yourself."

Claybourne did not back away. "I'll go on running this ranch the best way I know how," he said. "If you don't agree with my methods and what I do, that's your hard luck."

"You run the ranch to suit yourself," Jeff said, "but keep your gunslicks away from me. That's a warning, Claybourne."

"And if I don't?"

"It won't be only the men you sent I'll come gunning for, it will be you, too."

"Big talk for a nester," Claybourne murmured. "You're on borrowed time right now. You're lucky to be alive. All I have to do is yell and a half a dozen of my crew will be down on you."

"I expect you're right," Jeff said. "You look like the kind of man that always comes with plenty of help."

Riley Claybourne's face flushed. For the

first time Burkhart had got through to him, reached a touchy spot. "I can look after myself," he said stiffly.

"Good," Jeff said, "because right now you're my ticket out of here. I don't trust you or your hired gunslingers. You're walking out that door with me and riding right along at my side until I'm away from here."

"Not if I. . . ."

"Don't say something you can't back up. Only way you'll get out of doing it is for you to start something here and now. And I doubt if you're willing to try that."

Claybourne threw a quick glance at Cam Sutter. He looked down. "All right, I'll give the word you're to have an open trail."

"Not good enough," Jeff said at once. "You're going along. You're my insurance policy." He saw the alarm rising in the girl's eyes. "Don't worry, Miss Sutter, he won't get hurt unless he tries to cross me."

She bit at her lower lip in that nervous way of hers. "And your other promise?"

"I'll keep my part of the bargain." He reached forward, took Claybourne's gun from its holster, and handed it to the girl. "Reckon you'd best hold onto this for him. Might keep him from getting hurt."

"What other promise you talking about?"

Claybourne demanded, immediately suspicious.

"A matter between us," Cam Sutter replied coolly.

"I demand to know!" the foreman said, again angry. "Your father put me in charge of this ranch! I have a right to know what . . . !"

"Turn around. Head out that doorway," Burkhart cut in coldly. "No need my telling you a wrong move or word on your part will get you a bullet in the knee. Do just what I say."

Claybourne hesitated for only a moment. He wheeled angrily, strode through the opening onto the porch.

"Hold up right there," Burkhart ordered. He looked beyond the foreman. The same three men were at the hitching rail. They came to wary attention as Claybourne and Jeff came out onto the gallery.

"Tell one of them to get you a horse," Burkhart directed in a low voice.

Again Claybourne hesitated. Jeff pressed the muzzle of the Henry into his spine with a steady insistence.

"Bring me a horse, Chick!" the foreman said.

The cowboy addressed as Chick stared for a time, then turned and trotted off across the yard. Abilene Dow and the other rider moved a step closer, their hard, dour faces clouded into a frown.

"Tell them everything's all right. Tell them to go on about their business."

Claybourne placed his gaze upon Dow. "Forget it, Ab. You and Denver get on back to the bunkhouse."

The yard was suddenly hushed, tense. Dow shook his head slowly. "What's goin' on here, Riley? First you tell me. . . ."

"I said forget it!" Claybourne barked. "This joker's calling the turn right now. Be different another time."

"Maybe this is the time," Dow murmured.

Jeff Burkhart stepped carefully from behind Claybourne. His face was set and the full knowledge of trouble's immediate presence was upon him. It was a bad place for it to happen, but if Dow wanted it, this was the moment. He watched the gunman with narrowed eyes.

"You weren't so brave yesterday. What's fired you up today?"

The blond gunman stared at him vacantly. "Maybe yesterday wasn't my day. Maybe this is."

"Never a good time to die," Jeff said quietly.

"Something for you to be worryin' over,"

Dow replied. "I got things to square with you. . . ."

"You damned fool!" Claybourne suddenly exploded. "You want to get me killed? Now do what I told you! Forget it. Get on back to the bunkhouse and wait for me."

Dow's shoulders came down slowly. The man beside him wheeled about abruptly, shambled off across the yard. Dow, never taking his hating gaze off Burkhart, shrugged.

"I'll be comin' for you later, mister," he said, and moved off.

Chick came around the corner of the house at that moment, leading a horse for Claybourne. Burkhart waited until the cowboy had retreated toward the bunkhouse, and then prodded the foreman off the gallery.

"Mount up, slow and easy. And keep right on being smart. It's keeping you alive."

Claybourne made no reply. He stepped to the saddle and waited there, motionless. Jeff climbed onto his buckskin. He threw a quick glance to the bunkhouse, visible from that point. Four men now stood before its length, watched the proceedings with close interest.

"Guess you know, if they try to follow. . . ."

"They won't," Claybourne snapped.

"Come on, let's get this over with!"

Burkhart turned his attention to the main house. Cam Sutter was in the doorway, Claybourne's gun still in her hand.

"Good day, Miss Sutter," he said, touching the brim of his hat.

He waited until she nodded and then, herding the foreman ahead of him, rode out of the yard and started up the slope.

VIII

A half an hour later, Jeff released Riley Claybourne. There had been no attempt to pursue, so far as he could tell, but trusting no one, he waited until the foreman was gone from sight, then swung wide to a point where he could watch Sutter's ranch unobserved.

He saw Claybourne ride into the yard a few minutes later and pull to a stop before the bunkhouse. The four men Jeff had last seen standing in the yard appeared immediately. There was a brief exchange of conversation between the foreman and his riders after which Claybourne crossed the yard to the main house while the others turned and reëntered their own quarters. Jeff grinned his satisfaction and guided the buckskin back onto the trail. Apparently he had convinced Riley Claybourne; there would be no immediate pursuit.

He pointed the buckskin then for his own place, riding easily, taking his time. He was having his first good look at the land since his return and was finding a man's keen enjoyment in the beauty of it. Grass was thick; game was abundant on the wooded slopes.

It was wonderful country, a good place for a man to settle down and raise a family. He understood now why his father had chosen the Calaveras Hills to bring his family into, and strangely his thoughts immediately swung to Cam Sutter. What a wife she would make for a man! Her natural, unaffected beauty, the calm reasonableness of her, that cool determination that glowed in her eyes when she was aroused. A man couldn't ask for more.

He wondered if there was anything between her and Riley Claybourne. The foreman had exhibited a familiarity that would make it seem so. Yet Cam — what was her real name? — showed no particular kinship for him. Perhaps Riley Claybourne was presuming too much; Jeff decided he would like to know for certain.

He shook his head, considering his own thoughts. Did he believe he had a chance with Cam Sutter? He, a homesteader, at war with her and all her kind! What was wrong with him? The Sutters, to all intents and purposes, were his sworn enemies. She would have little time for him — just as he should have none for her.

He reached his place late in the afternoon, after several hours of aimless wandering through the hills. Pete Langford was busy at the necessary daily chores, and, after stabling the buckskin, Jeff fell to and did his share. Langford asked no questions until they were again finished with the evening meal and sat in the little parlor.

"You mean you just up and rode right into Ben Sutter's place?" the old man asked after he heard Jeff's first remarks.

"How else you figure I'd get to see him? Had to go there, didn't I?"

"Maybe you got more gall than sense," Langford muttered. "Ridin' in like that with them feelin' the way they would after you blasted one of their prime gunslingers . . . well, it was a crazy thing to do, that's all I can say. You get to talk to Sutter?"

"No. He was asleep. Talked to his daughter."

Langford eyed him sharply. "So, what'd she have to say about it? Claimed she didn't know nothin', I'll bet."

"She found it hard to believe," Jeff admitted, coming back to the moment. "Said she didn't think her father was aware of such goings on, either. That running the ranch was left up to Claybourne."

"And you believed that? What happened then?"

"She said she would talk it over with her father, tell him what I had to say. Then she'll ride over here tomorrow and let me know what he wants to do about it."

"Just talk!" Langford exclaimed. "Ain't no truth in it. And don't you be holdin' your breath till she shows up tomorrow."

Jeff swung his attention to Langford. "Why?"

"That gal won't be comin' over here. First place, Ben Sutter won't let her. Neither will Claybourne. They ain't about to let that little red-headed filly upset their plans."

Burkhart considered that. "You figure Sutter knows all about what his crew is doing then?"

"You're damned well right he does!" Langford shouted, his face rising to a high flush. "And don't you go gettin' any ideas he don't! You been fooled, boy, fooled good! You stuck out your neck this day and all for nothin'!"

"Maybe," Burkhart said quietly. "I still

figure I'll hear from Cam Sutter. And she'll talk to her pa. I'd bet on that, too."

"She's Ben Sutter's kid," Langford answered, wagging his head. "She'll stand by him. Maybe she don't know all that goes on, but it won't make no difference. She's a Sutter and that's the way she'll think."

"I would expect that," Jeff said. "Point is . . . *does* Ben Sutter know what's going on?"

The older man snorted. "Sutter never got big like he is by singin' psalms to his neighbors. He's a thievin', grabbin' skunk. What he can't get his paws on one way, he'll get another. You can take my word for that."

"Could be," Burkhart said. "But we'll wait until we hear from Cam Sutter before we do anything." He paused, waited out a minute. "You know if there's anything between the girl and Claybourne? Like maybe them getting married, I mean?"

Pete Langford's expression changed, became stolid. He studied Jeff thoughtfully for a long minute. Then: "Be hard to say. Riley stands mighty high in that family. Expect there is somethin' like that in the wind. Be plumb natural, what with Ben dependin' on Riley the way he does." He stopped, considered Burkhart thoroughly once more. "Why?"

"I was just wondering."

"You ain't maybe gettin' some ideas about that little filly, are you?"

Jeff made no answer. He drew forth the sack of tobacco with its thin sheaf of papers, rolled himself a cigarette.

"It'd sure be one way to ask for more trouble," Langford said. "Sort of like puttin' a fox in a chicken yard."

"Forget it!" Jeff snapped, feeling a strange anger rise within him. Immediately he regretted his hasty words. "Never mind, Pete. I was just wondering about the girl and Claybourne." He arose, got himself a drink of water from the bucket and tin dipper. "Made it good and plain to Claybourne today that we'd stand no more foolishness from him and his hired guns," he said, moving restlessly about the room.

"You figure he paid you any mind?"

"Who would know? But he did a lot of listening. He knows what he can expect if he sends that bunch down here again. Told him I'd be right after him."

Langford chuckled. "Riley'd understand that kind of talk. That's the way he is. And don't figure him for no soft-headed greenhorn. Riley's been around. He can skin his own cats, it come needful. Maybe he sort of dandies hisself up some but he's all man

73

underneath."

"Guessed that. Just from the way he handled those gunslicks of his."

"That'd be him, all right. Tough as they come but smart. Could be he's takin' a squint at his hole card now, howsomever. First time he's come up against a man tough as hisself."

"It's a game anybody can play at, if he's willing," Jeff said.

"And got the sand for it," Langford added. "Well, reckon it's about time to turn in. You be around in the mornin'? There's a few things ought to be done. Chores around a place like this can sure get ahead of a man."

"I'll be here," Jeff said. "You tell me what needs to be done, and I'll get at it. Got to do something about that barn, too. And while we're talking, Pete, I don't see any reason for you to be living out there in that shack you built. Might as well move in here with me."

Langford scratched at his chin. "I'm sure obliged, Jeff. Maybe I'll just do that. Fact is, your pa mentioned it once or twice. Trouble is a man gets used to bunkin' alone and it's kind of hard to change."

"It'd be better if we were together, should there come a raid some night."

"Reckon that's right," Langford said, nodding his head. "I'll see about it tomorrow. G'night."

"Good night," Jeff said, and watched the old man shuffle through the doorway into the night.

The advisability of their being together in event of trouble had appeared to him only at that exact moment. He had been thinking first of how lonely a man could get in a house by himself.

IX

It was just after daybreak when Jeff and Pete Langford finished their breakfast and headed toward the barn, ready to begin the early morning chores. The sky was clear, the air sharp with the first promises of fall weather in the offing.

They fell to work at once accomplishing the various tasks that needed to be done. An hour later Pete Langford halted Jeff at a job of transferring hay to the loft where it could more easily be thrown down to the stock.

"Reckon that can wait, Jeff. Just happened to remember there's about a half a dozen yearlin's down in the west pasture that's got to be moved. Expect they've pretty near grazed that patch of ground down to bedrock."

Burkhart stood his long-tined fork in a corner of the building. "Where you want them moved to?"

"I was thinkin' they ought to be down in that holler about a half mile east of where they are. Grass is real good there. Howsomever, you take a look for yourself. You're runnin' this outfit now. Maybe you've got some ideas of your own."

Jeff pivoted to the stall where the buckskin was bedded. He saddled him quickly, took up the short-barreled Henry that he had earlier hung on a peg near the doorway where it would have been handy in case of unexpected visitors.

"Time you finish movin' them yearlin's, I'll be done here," Langford said. "Then maybe we can start diggin' around in that barn, seein' if there's anything worth keepin'."

Burkhart nodded, swung to the saddle. He started down the short runway, passed through the open door into the growing sunlight — and came to a sudden halt.

"Somebody's coming!" he called over his shoulder.

He heard Langford throw aside the rake, or whatever he held in his hands, and trot up behind him. There was a metallic *click* as Jeff cocked his rifle. A half a dozen riders entered the far end of the yard, curved for the house. They saw him then, sitting on the buckskin before the barn, altered their course and came straight on.

"Sutter's bunch?" Jeff wondered. "One of them looks like Claybourne."

From nearby Langford said: "Claybourne, sure enough. And a couple of his boys. But that feller beside him, that's Harry Wade, the marshal. And the fat one, he's Vic Antrum, his deputy."

Jeff Burkhart's hand came away from the rifle, already tucked in its scabbard under his leg. He watched the riders approach, a frown on his face. Claybourne — and the law. Why were they teamed up?

The riders halted, spread out in a line facing Burkhart and Pete Langford. Harry Wade was a middle-aged man with a square, unsmiling face. He brushed at his mustache.

"You Burkhart?"

Jeff nodded. He let his glance touch the others: Claybourne, silent and expressionless; Abilene Dow, the blond gunman, his gray lips pulled down into a sneer; Antrum, the other two riders, both strangers to him but apparently not from the B-Bar-S.

"You're coming with me. You're under arrest."

"Arrest?" Burkhart echoed in surprise. He threw a hot glance at Claybourne. "What kind of a deal is this? Arrest for what?"

"For killing Ben Sutter," Wade said quietly.

Jeff Burkhart sat completely still in the dead silence that dropped across the yard. Ben Sutter dead — murdered! The import of that struck him, turned him again toward Riley Claybourne.

"Why me? This some of your doing?"

The foreman made no reply. He met Burkhart's stare, gave it back with a steady, glowing hatred.

Wade said: "This is my doing, Burkhart. I'm making the charge, considering what happened yesterday."

"Now, just what did happen yesterday?" Jeff demanded, anger rising within him.

"I know you went to see Ben Sutter. You were all het up over the trouble that's between the two of you. Mad enough to kill . . . which you don't mind doing. . . ."

"If you mean Animas and Searles, they. . . ."

"I know," Wade cut in smoothly, "it was a fair fight. You had plenty of witnesses. I can't take you in for that. But the fact remains, you went over to Sutter's that next

78

morning ready to settle your bitch with him. Only you didn't get to him. His daughter saw to that."

"He was sleeping. She said he had been given some laudanum and she couldn't wake him up. All I went there for was to talk. I wanted to see if we couldn't straighten this thing out before it got worse. His daughter said she would talk to him about it and let me know."

"I know all that," Wade said. "You told her you'd wait until you heard from her before you did anything more. Only you changed your mind. You didn't wait. You dropped back last night after everybody was in bed and murdered Ben Sutter."

"That's a damned lie, Harry!" Pete Langford shouted. "That boy never left this place all night!"

Wade's calm eyes shifted to the old man. "You right sure of that, Pete? You with him all the time?"

Langford stalled out a few moments, looking down at his feet. "Well, reckon I was sleepin' some. But I sure would have heard him leave. . . ."

"Maybe," the lawman said.

Jeff Burkhart shook his head. "I never murdered Sutter, Marshal. And Pete is right. I didn't leave here last night. Not for a minute. You're making a big mistake taking me in."

Wade shrugged. "Don't think so. You had plenty of reasons for wanting Ben Sutter dead."

"You could say that, I guess. Sutter's men killed my pa, burned half the place down. That's cause enough to make any man act. But I had an idea. . . ."

"My point, exactly. You had good reasons. You made that clear to everybody. I figure your own talking gives me sufficient cause to hold you until the circuit judge shows up."

"You think I'd gun down a cripple, a man who couldn't defend himself?" Burkhart demanded, anger suddenly boilng over. "Use your head, Marshal. Somebody else is back of this and they're real interested in making it look like it was all my doing."

"Well, you was for sure honin' to gun down somebody yesterday!" Abilene Dow broke in. "Figure'd we'd seen the last of Riley here when you rode off into the brush holdin' a gun at his back!"

"What's that?" Wade demanded sharply. He swung to Claybourne. "Something you never told me, Riley."

The foreman shrugged. "Didn't think it was necessary, considering the evidence you already had. When Burkhart there left the ranch, he put a gun on me and forced me to ride on ahead. Said it was to guarantee him safe passage. I don't know if that was really it or if he planned to kill me but changed his mind."

"You know damned well what I meant!" Burkhart snapped. "The only way I could ride out of that nest of scorpions without getting stung. I was looking for a bullet in my back every step of the way!"

"Never mind," Wade said. "We'll let the judge do the deciding. . . ."

"Get out of here, boy!" Pete Langford's voice suddenly shouted. "They got you framed tight!"

Jeff felt the buckskin lunge forward under him as Langford cracked the horse smartly across the rump with his hat.

"I'll hold 'em quiet till you make it out of sight!"

The buckskin swerved, headed for the corner of the barn. Behind him Jeff heard Wade's outraged cry.

"Throw down that gun, Pete! You're interfering with the law!"

"Don't nobody make a move!" Langford's high, cracked voice warned. "I'll blast the first man that tries anything!"

The buckskin rounded the corner of the

barn at a dead run, lengthened his stride as he headed for a grove of trees a quarter mile distant. Maybe it was better this way, Jeff thought, although running away would make it appear that he was guilty of Ben Sutter's death. But at least he would be free to move about, dig into the matter, and have a chance to come up with the real killer, thus clearing himself.

He glanced ahead. First he would have to find a place to hide. Wade would not be long in organizing a posse and putting it on his trail. He recalled then a place where, as a boy, he often went. It was a well-hidden ledge, high up on the purple-shaded ridge back of the valley.

He probed through his memory, searching for his knowledge of the trail and where he could most easily reach it. Once on the ridge he would be well out of sight, could look down and observe the activities below.

X

He saw first sign of the posse late that morning.

Four riders working up the valley just west of his place. They moved slowly, little more than dark blurs at such great distance. Half an hour later he saw another line of searchers, seven or eight this time, crawling with extreme care and caution out of the south.

Evidently Harry Wade had recruited more posse members in Riflestock. Or possibly Riley Claybourne had placed his entire crew from the B-Bar-S at the lawman's disposal. At any rate, it was a large company of men that sought him. It reminded Jeff Burkhart of the war, of the times when he lay hidden on a Virginia hilltop or deep in a Georgia swamp and watched Rebel soldiers scour the country for him and others. This was no less deadly. A bullet fired in peace would kill a man every bit as quickly as one fired in war. And those riders far below would shoot him down, if they discovered him, just as readily as any soldier in gray.

But they were not likely to find him; he was far west of the area through which they searched, and high above them. They would not suspect he had ridden immediately to that point where, once upon it, there was no escape except down the same indefinite trail. They would assume he ducked into the brush and dense groves of the near badlands that fronted the ridge. There, pursuing any man's normal thoughts, he would head northward under such ideal cover and make his way until, at least, he reached the towering wilds of Colorado. That's what they, were they in his position, would do.

If so, more posse members should be moving in from the north, he realized. There would be a rush to cut in ahead of him, seal him off. He turned his attention to that direction, let his gaze probe the area thoroughly. Minutes later he saw that he was right. There were riders, a half a dozen or more, pressing in from that section. Marshal Harry Wade's strategy became clear — a three-pronged advance through the breaks would be made. The triad would converge eventually at the base of the ridge; he, presumably, would be driven before the onmarching lines, trapped in a neat pocket against the mountain from which there would be no escape.

The afternoon came, began to wear on. The small specks that were men and horses grew larger, but with painful slowness. At the rate they traveled, it would be well beyond dark by the time they joined forces. His thoughts came to a full stop; when they did, what would they do upon discovering their net empty?

Would they turn, retrace their steps? Would they abandon the search, concluding he had, in some manner, slipped through their fingers? Or would they break up into pairs and begin a new quest? If so, some would remember there was a trail that led to the top of the rise and sooner or later he would be discovered. He could be easily trapped at the top of that trail.

That he could keep them off as long as his ammunition for Little Henry held out was apparent. But the thought of that — of killing townspeople he did not know, who had no interest in the matter other than seeing that the law was served — did not appeal to him. He had not slunk through the night like a cowardly cat and killed Ben Sutter; it seemed unthinkable and criminal to him that he should kill anyone to prove the fact.

He must get off the ledge. That became more apparent to him as the minutes dragged by. He must not allow himself to become trapped on the rocky shelf where he lay with no way out except down the trail — and straight into the arms of the posse. But it would be better to wait, hold off until the three lines of riders were nearer. Then he could slip off the ridge, gamble on his ability to work through the line of searchers unseen. He had done it before, many times, during the war. This should be little different.

He lay then, watched the men approach — but his mind was not upon them. He was wondering about Ben Sutter, who killed him, and why? There were many men with motive enough. Pick out any of the homesteaders or small ranchers the huge B-Bar-S had swallowed up. All could be suspects.

And there were others, those who stood to gain. His train of thought halted at that; leading the list of those would be Riley Claybourne. He already ran the vast, sprawling Sutter empire as his own. With Ben Sutter out of the way, he could virtually make his control complete, actually take it over. Cam would present no problem. She would readily recognize the fact that she could not operate the huge spread without Claybourne's iron fist to back her up. She would need Riley Claybourne.

Claybourne was a slick operator. There was no overlooking that fact. Jeff recalled how effectively he had brought to bear, in his favor, the incident at Sutter's ranch that previous day. He had intentionally avoided mentioning how Jeff had taken him virtual prisoner, forced him to ride off as a means for protection. And when it was related to Harry Wade, it carried double impact. The foreman was smart — and cunning as a fox.

Everything would work out nicely for Mr. Claybourne. Ben Sutter would be gone, out of the picture for all time; his only opposition would be in jail, destined to hang for the rancher's murder. And Cam, caught up in the middle, would be the innocent pawn. Either she would become the wife of Riley Claybourne, or she would not. It wouldn't really matter to the foreman. The net result would be the same; B-Bar-S would fall neatly into his hands.

Jeff wondered if Cam had heard anything out of the ordinary when her father was killed. And how was it done? A knife, for silence — or had it been a bullet coming out of the dark? He wished he might see her, talk to her, and get the answers to a few questions that were gathering in his mind. Perhaps, if he could persuade her to tell him all she knew of the hours before Ben Sutter's death, he might get some idea of who the murderer was.

He noticed then that the riders to the east had halted. They had not pulled in together but had simply stopped, as if waiting. He saw one man cut away and strike off to the south, intending apparently to meet the men coming up from that direction. Wade was doing the expected thing; he would unite all three posses when they drew near the ridge.

Jeff studied the groups of men below. It was too soon to start down the trail. Moving along the face of the mountain he could easily be seen. He would have to wait until the men were nearer, closer to the base. Then brush and bulging rock formations and the natural contours of the mountain itself would seal off their view of him.

That would cut it pretty fine — he realized that a moment later. It would increase the odds against his slipping by them. But it would be dark by that time, and that would help immeasurably. A man could move easily and safely through the night if he used care.

He turned around, glanced toward the sun. An hour or less and it would drop beyond the ridge; another and it would set. That would be the moment to start out.

He would get the buckskin — well hidden now in the brush a third of the way up the trail — and swing toward the south. Brush was thicker in that particular section. And there was a fairly deep wash that he could travel down. Not only would he be less likely seen but the loose, fine sand on the floor of the arroyo would effectively muffle the buckskin's hoofs.

Once past the posse, he would head for Sutter's ranch. He would be taking a long chance, gambling that most of the B-Bar-S crew were with Wade — but he had to see Cam Sutter; he must talk to her.

Maybe then he could turn up something that would convince her he was not the killer, could come up with something that would clear him of the charge now hanging over him. And it would save Cam.

XI

With the coming of darkness some of the posse members departed. They would be the family men, those who had chores to perform or businesses to look after and who had volunteered their services only for the period of time they could spare. Jeff Burkhart, high on the ridge, watched them ride off — six, perhaps seven men.

He lay on his perch, saw the watch fires blaze into life, and this, too, took him back to the war and the innumerable times he had looked upon such a scene. There were two dozen or more of the flickering orange spots in the increasing darkness, spaced evenly before the ridge in a generous semi-circle. When he could no longer distinguish men from shadows, he got to his feet and started down the trail that scarred the face of the cliff.

He moved silently but fast, finding no difficulty in descending the mountain. He reached the lower area and cut off to his right, headed for the hidden box cañon where he had concealed the buckskin. The horse welcomed him with an impatient bobbing of his long head and a low nicker. Burkhart quickly quieted him but he was not particularly worried about being heard. The posses were a considerable distance away and unless some members were on the mountain itself, ascending the trail, there was little danger of their noticing such sounds.

Burkhart, however, was taking no rash chances. There was always the possibility that someone, or even a small party, might think of the trail and decide to investigate it. Accordingly he led the buckskin out of the deep slash and finished the balance of sloping distance still on foot, keeping well into the brush that skirted the pathway.

His recollection of the land was good. He came out almost immediately at the mouth of the sandy wash. He halted there to listen, to consider. It would not be easy from that point on. The chances of blundering into a man wandering about in the dark, or of meeting up with a guard stationed by Harry Wade, were very real. But it was a gamble he would have to take.

With his hand on the buckskin's bridle, he started down the narrow, brushy wash.

There was only the pale light of the stars for illumination and for that he was grateful.

The first hundred yards passed without incident. Back, behind him and to his left, he could hear the low drone of men's voices. Ahead there was only silence. This disturbed him somewhat. It was inconceivable that Wade would leave the ends of his half circle open and unguarded. Yet he could see no fire's glow or hear any sounds that would indicate there were men somewhere farther along. There should be a campfire, for the night was blowing, cool and sharp, with a good breeze coming in from the north. And he should hear men talking. There was neither, and, being a man of logical mind, Jeff became instantly wary, alert for something unexpected.

He completed the first quarter mile, perhaps a bit less. The arroyo was wider, deeper at this point with thicker stands of brush and small trees scattered with much closer regularity. Now it might be advisable to mount the buckskin in the interests of removing himself from the area of the mountain as quickly as possible. He must be beyond Wade's ring of sentries by now. And the wash was of sufficient depth for a man, riding a horse, to move without being silhouetted above the skyline. He rounded a sharp turn, deciding he would go to the saddle — and came face to face with a man.

For a brief moment both were too surprised to do more than stare. Then Jeff Burkhart, knowing his life depended on the outcome of the next minutes, lunged at the rider. He could not afford a gunshot, or permit the man to cry out; either would bring others down upon him instantly.

He struck the man full on. They went over in an explosion of dust. The posse member grunted as breath was torn from his lungs but he lashed out with his rifle, using the butt as a club. It grazed Burkhart's jaw, did no damage. He slapped it aside, knocked it from the struggling man's grasp.

Jeff fought silently, desperately, smashing his fists into the cowboy's face and body, seeking to get in a telling blow that would knock him out. They rolled back and forth on the sandy floor of the arroyo, a threshing, squirming tangle of legs and arms and heaving bodies.

Jeff felt the man's knotted hands drive into him with powerful force. Whoever he was, he was strong and husky, and after the first violent minute Burkhart knew he had his work cut out for him. He began to worry about the racket they were setting up. The harsh rasping of their breathing, the dry *clatter* when they reeled into the brush seemed abnormally loud. The noise was bound to attract other men and that thought spurred him to bring the fight to a finish as quickly as possible.

He could get no force behind his blows. Prone or on his knees, he seemed to lack the power it required to knock the cowboy senseless. He drove a hail of short rights to the man's belly, tore himself free as the fingers clutching his left arm relaxed. He bounded to his feet just as the cowboy got to his knees. He aimed a hard right to the man's head. The cowboy dodged, rolled away, and was upright in a quick blur of movement.

"Over here!" he suddenly yelled. "I got him . . . over here!"

Burkhart surged forward. He sank his left hand into the man's unprotected belly again. He followed with a whistling right that landed fully on the ear. The cowboy rocked uncertainly on his heels. Burkhart drove in mercilessly. He straightened the cowboy up with a sharp left to the face, crossed quickly with another right that caught the man on the jaw. The cowboy began to wilt.

"Hey . . . over here . . . !"

Jeff stilled his summons with a blow that cracked like a whip when it struck. The cowboy spun half about, went to his knees. He hung there for a brief time, head sagging forward on his chest, toppled over with a deep sigh.

Jeff wheeled and raced the dozen steps to where the buckskin waited. He could hear men running, crashing through the heat-dried brush, coming in answer to the cowboy's frantic call. He reached down, snatched up his rifle from where he had dropped it. With Little Henry in hand, he vaulted into the saddle.

He heeled the buckskin's ribs, sent him forward in a startled lunge. They thundered down the brush-strewn arroyo, heedless of the noise they made. Yells broke out behind them. There was a bright flash of light as a gun shattered the night. Jeff heard no drone of lead and stayed his own urge to shoot back. His exact position was unknown to them; they were aiming blindly. He twisted back around in the saddle, his thumb and finger relaxing on the Henry's hammer and trigger. He bent low over the buckskin's outthrust neck, reducing the possibilities of being seen. They covered a short, straight run in the sandy wash, then turned sharply left once more.

Immediately ahead there was a blur of motion. Burkhart realized it was another posse member, mounted this time, coming to investigate the confusion. The buckskin swerved to avoid a collision. He stumbled, almost went down.

"Who's that?" the oncoming rider yelled, fighting with his startled horse.

"Back there . . . they got him!" Burkhart answered.

"No . . . !" the man shouted, suddenly aware. "You're him!"

Burkhart threw himself to one side, offering no target. The buckskin, still having trouble with his footing in the loose sand and scattered rocks and brush, veered left, then to the right. Burkhart, striving to get set for a snap shot, was almost hurled from the saddle. He caught at the horn, righted himself as the buckskin recovered and rushed on.

Almost directly ahead of him he saw the posse rider. He had whirled about, now drove in at an angle, hoping to cut off the buckskin. A gun flash burst in Burkhart's eyes and his horse again swerved sharply. He threw his own answering bullet at the crouched shape in front of him, reined the buckskin in tightly, and forced him head-on at the other rider.

They were at close quarters. He lashed out with the Henry, using it as a club. He felt the stinging shock of contact as it connected. He heard a grunt of pain, an oath. There was another burst of orange light. Burkhart felt a bullet sear through his leg about halfway between knee and hip.

He brought his rifle around for another shot but the horses, frenzied by the explosion so nearby, were plunging away in opposite directions, their speed carrying them quickly apart. Jeff flung a hasty glance over his shoulder. The rider was doubled forward. He seemed almost to fall from his saddle.

Burkhart did not slow the buckskin, but let him race on down the wash. The blindly aimed blow apparently had been a lucky one. He had not been so fortunate himself.

XII

There were no immediate sounds of pursuit. Jeff Burkhart, however, was not misled by that knowledge. It would take several minutes for posse members, caught on foot, to get mounted. Then they would come sweeping down from the mountain's base in a widely flung line, hoping to keep him before

them and eventually run him into the
ground.

He clutched at his throbbing leg, allowed
the buckskin to run on freely through the
night. Wade would expect him to continue
on the course he had taken, due south. It
was a land of brush and rock-filled arroyos,
choppy hills, and small cañons. It offered
many hiding places and a vast amount of
protective cover for a man seeking to throw
others off his trail. They would figure he
was going deep into it.

To his left and to his right, the plains
country unrolled in long, almost continual
flats. Probably they would not expect him
to expose himself in such open country. And
it could be a foolhardy move. But he had a
good start on them, and, if he could swing
off, get out from in front of their forage-line
formation before it came rushing off the
slope, he might possibly elude them. He
must stop soon. The wound in his leg was
not too serious but it required certain
minimum attention. He was losing too
much blood.

Coming to a decision, he curved the
buckskin off to his left, choosing that direction rather than the other since it would
place him in the proper area for continuing
on to Sutter's B-Bar-S Ranch. He was still

determined to talk with Cam, see if he could come up with an idea as to who the killer was. He knew he must find the answer soon for, until he did, his own life was worth less than nothing. Harry Wade would never rest until he had brought Burkhart down.

The buckskin began to slow, to tire. He pulled the horse down to a good trot, always keeping to the low swales and shallow dips as he crossed the wide flats. A dark smudge of trees loomed up far ahead. He chose that as a destination point, bore steadily for it, turning about occasionally to examine his back trail for pursuers.

He saw no one following, and to his relief he heard the riders in the distance, speeding southward. It had been a lucky break, catching them dismounted. The ensuing delay while they caught up their horses and swung to the saddle had meant the difference in escape and capture for Jeff Burkhart.

He reached the grove of cottonwoods, pulled off to one side at once. He chose a spot where he could still watch the flats, just in case Wade had sent riders fanning out from the main party. He dismounted, secured the buckskin to a staunch shrub.

The leg wound was not serious, as he had suspected. It had bled considerably — but that, he remembered from the war, was a good thing. It had cleansed itself to some degree by doing so. But still it should be dressed now — and some antiseptic applied to prevent infection.

Jeff had no answer for that need. With his bandanna he improvised a bandage and bound the folded cloth into place. For now it made a satisfactory arrangement. It would have to be just that and no more. Actual medical care could wait — but not for long.

He mounted the buckskin and headed off through the grove, taking his directions from the high, dark bulk of the ridge now far to his left. He rode steadily, not pushing his horse hard but holding him to a consistent pace. When three hours later, he rode into the valley where Ben Sutter's buildings lay, he was still surviving, despite the loss of blood and intense pangs of hunger shooting from an empty stomach.

It was late — not far from midnight, he guessed. He would be lucky to find Cam Sutter still up. But even if she had retired, he would arouse her. Seeing and talking to her was of the greatest importance. When he drew near the buildings, he saw there was no cause to worry about that part of it. Lights still burned in the main house as well as in the crew's quarters. He circled wide, going to the far edge of the yard, keeping the buckskin in the deeper shadows as much as possible.

He located a large clump of shrubbery — lilac or some sort of flowering bush — pulled in behind it and came to a halt. There he dismounted and tied the horse, electing to go farther on foot. It would be much easier to duck out of sight, if someone unexpectedly presented himself.

That emergency arose almost immediately. He heard the soft *thud* of approaching horses, walking slowly into the yard. He was caught in the open, halfway across the clearing that surrounded the house. He dropped to a crouched position, his injured leg shrieking with pain at the sudden twist he subjected it to.

There were two riders. They entered the yard not thirty feet away, pointed for the kitchen. Evidently some of the night crew working nearby, dropping in for a cup of coffee. Burkhart held himself rigid, scarcely daring to breathe. If he could remain absolutely still, they would pass him by, taking him, perhaps, for a clump of brush in the meager starlight.

". . . had him pinned down somewhere in the brush near the ridge," the words of one of the riders came to Burkhart.

He watched the pair gain the corner of

100

the building, pass on out of sight. He relaxed slightly, not rising but remaining in his crouched position until he heard the side door slam. Then he rose to his feet and, ignoring his protesting leg, ran the remainder of the distance to the house.

He was on the south side of the structure. Lamplight shone from a window near the center and he took quick calculation of its location. He recalled what he could of the house's arrangement: the parlor off which a short hallway led — Ben Sutter had occupied a room at the end. The light seemed to be in a room between the front and rear. Likely that was Cam's bedroom.

He moved toward that window, hoping there would be space enough around the drawn shade to permit him to look inside. He worked his way along the smoothly plastered wall, came at last to the framed opening. A small area near the base was open. He peered through that, saw Cam Sutter. She was dressed for sleeping but had delayed. She sat in a chair near a table, was thumbing through a thick book, an album of pictures, he thought it was.

He considered the wisdom of tapping on the glass but discarded the idea at once. Feeling as she did, she would not care to see him or talk to him. Likely she would raise an alarm and bring some of the crew swarming down upon him. It would be better to take her by surprise, by force, if need be, and compel her to give him a chance to speak.

He continued on along the structure to its fronting end and crossed to the entrance. Praying that the door was not locked, he tried the latch. It came open to his touch and he slipped inside. He paused then, removed his spurs, fearing they might jingle and give him away. He laid them on the table that stood near the center of the parlor and started down the short hallway. A rectangle of light broke its length about halfway along.

He reached that and again halted. Outside he heard the flat *slap* of a door swinging shut. He waited, tension beginning to build within him as he considered the possibility of Riley Claybourne or some other member of the Sutter crew coming to the main house for one reason or another. A long minute dragged by. Two. Three. He heard nothing more. He turned his attention back to the girl.

He looked cautiously around the facing. Cam sat with her back toward him. Again he considered attracting her attention and once more he put it aside as being unwise.

He disliked the idea of frightening her but it appeared to be the only way.

He glided softly into the room, moving with the superb skill of a hard-trained Army scout. He came up behind her, paused. Then, with a quick, encircling motion of his arms, he clamped one hand upon her lips, pinning her against the back of the chair with the other.

XIII

Cam Sutter struggled violently for a few moments as surprise and terror gripped her. She relaxed gradually, going limply into the chair. Burkhart released the arm that bound her about the waist. Still keeping her lips tightly compressed, he moved forward until she could see who he was. Her eyes spread into large circles of fear and wonder when she recognized him.

He shook his head. "Sorry to scare you, ma'am, but it was the only way. I was afraid you'd call out and bring some of your crew down on my neck."

She frowned, endeavored to say something but her words were only a distorted murmur of sound.

"Don't be scared of me. I'm not here to hurt you, only to talk. I didn't kill your father. I'm just trying to find out who did."

Again she tried to say something. She twisted her head far to one side but his fingers would not relax their imprisoning grip. She gave it up after a bit, sank deeper into the chair.

He said: "That's better. If I take my hand away, will you keep quiet . . . not yell? I just want to ask you a couple of questions, then I'll be on my way."

She studied him for a moment, her eyes dark now in the lamplight. She nodded then. He removed his hand, released her.

She sprang to her feet at once. "You dare to come here!"

"One thing I had to do," he said, watching her warily. If she started to cry out, he would have to stop her. "Think a bit. It ought to prove to you that I had nothing to do with your father's death. I sure wouldn't risk coming here if I did. I would be a long way out of this country. And I had the chance, a good one, earlier today."

She stared at him, her face flushed, her shape rigid beneath the light robe she wore. The angry flare in her eyes began to die. She looked more closely at him, at the blood-stained bandage around his thigh. The stiff lines at the corners of her mouth softened.

"You've been hurt. . . ."

He shrugged. "No more than a scratch. Met up with the marshal and his posse back a ways." He wheeled, walked to the door, closed it softly. "Reckon you had no cause to think I'd keep my promise to you," he said, returning to her, "but for what it's worth, I did. I didn't know anything about Ben Sutter's death until the marshal and some others showed up at my place to take me in."

"Well," she said, doubt threading her voice, "you are the only one who had reason enough. Your own father getting shot down by a man who worked for my father . . . us. I guess I couldn't have blamed you."

"My quarrel there was with Carl Animas, only partly with your father. And if it had been with Ben Sutter, it would have been handled in the same way . . . not in the dark." He paused, waited for her to say something. When she did not, he added: "Can you tell me what all happened here last night?"

She lowered her glance. She half turned and her hand went to the book on the table. For a time she toyed with its edge. Then: "I was here, in this room. It was late, about this time, and I had already turned down the lamp. I heard a shot. It came from the outside, from the yard somewhere. And about the same time there was the sound of breaking glass."

"Breaking glass?" Burkhart repeated.

She said: "Yes. If it hadn't been for that, I probably wouldn't have thought anything about the shot. I got up, went to the parlor, but everything was all right there. I then ran to my father's room, at the end of the hall. He was dead. Someone had fired a bullet through the window and killed him as he lay there reading."

A slight tremor shook her. Jeff Burkhart, without thinking, stepped close, took her into his arms, seeking to comfort her. She did not pull away but pressed her head against his chest and began to sob quietly.

"It has all been so terrible! I still can't realize that it has happened, that it is true."

He patted her shoulder consolingly. "A thing like this is always hard to take . . . to understand. Seems your pa had already seen his share of grief without this happening, too. But a man never knows. Sometimes I think things are just meant to be and nothing is going to change them."

"He was so unhappy, being crippled up the way he was. And there was always the pain. . . ."

"He's out of that now," Burkhart said.

"And being the kind of man I figure he was, I expect he's glad of it now. . . ."

"He hated being dependent on anyone," she said.

"That's what I meant."

They stood there in the center of the small room for several minutes longer. Burkhart, feeling the press of time, said: "It was a bullet from the dark. Didn't the shot arouse anyone else? Some of the crew?"

She drew back from him, seemingly aware for the first time of what she was doing. "Yes, several of the men came running to this side of the house. They searched for a long time but they didn't find anybody."

"Who got here first?"

He waited out the moments while she thought, knowing her reply could mean much, or very little.

"I think it was Riley . . . Riley Claybourne, our foreman. I'm not sure."

"Is there any reason why he might get here sooner than the others? Are his quarters closer?"

She said: "A little."

That could be the reason, Burkhart had to admit. But it still did not quell the suspicions that gnawed steadily at him.

"You say you weren't the one who did it," Cam said then, her voice faltering a little.

"Who do you think it could have been?"

"It could have been any one of several although I can't see any of the homesteaders taking matters into their own hands. From what I hear, most of them moved out of the country, anyway. I've got a few hunches and ideas of my own but they will take a little proving." He stopped short, looked directly at her. "One thing I've got to be sure of . . . you don't think I did it?"

She shook her head slowly. "No, Jeff, I don't think you did. I guess I never really did, either. It was only that everything pointed your way. . . ."

"Or somebody made it look like it."

"Yes. I didn't want to think it was you, not after we had talked things over."

He moved to her, again took her slender form into the circle of his arms. "You ought to know, Cam, I could never do anything to hurt you. Not even if it cost me everything I own or expect to own in this world."

She tipped her face up to him. He bent quickly, pressed a kiss upon her lips, and for a long minute they remained that way, lost in the wonder of it all. He let his arms fall and stepped back, suddenly aware again of time.

"It's getting late. Somebody from the marshal's posse is bound to swing by here, and before I see Wade again, I want to have something to tell him." He halted, frowned, his dark features lost in deep study. "That foreman of yours. . . ."

He heard the faint *click* of the door's latch behind him. He whirled, or started to. The sudden shift of weight onto his injured leg took him unexpectedly. The leg buckled and he went to one knee. He flung a glance to the open door.

Riley Claybourne faced him, gun in hand.

XIV

A gasp escaped Cam Sutter's lips. She stepped back against the wall. Her hand flew to her throat.

"You all right, Cam?" Claybourne asked, coming forward a step. He did not remove his eyes from Burkhart, watching him with a steady, driving hatred.

"I'm all right," she said, recovering herself. "You can put that gun away. He didn't kill my father."

The foreman's heavy brows lifted. "Oh? He's convinced you of that?"

"You know I didn't," Burkhart said in a low voice.

Claybourne shook his head. "Fact is, I'm sure you did. And so is the marshal and everybody else around here."

"But I *know* he didn't!" the girl insisted.

"Why? Because he says so? You take the word of a killer, a man who hated your father, and believe it over all the evidence that points to the truth?" Claybourne shrugged impatiently. "Think straight, Cam. Who else could have done it?"

"You for a start on the list," Burkhart cut in coolly.

Claybourne's eyes flared. His mouth sagged. "Me?" he echoed. "You're loco, Burkhart. I've heard some crazy things but that beats them all."

"You've practically taken over Ben Sutter's ranch as it is. With him out of the way, it would be easy to finish the job."

Riley Claybourne smiled but there was a big anger in his eyes that belied the expression on his face. "You don't talk yourself out of this, Burkhart. Maybe you can make Cam think you're in the clear . . . but not me. I'm taking you straight to the marshal."

"No," the girl broke in, "I won't have it!"

"You don't have anything to say about it now," the foreman replied. "It's in the hands of the law. The marshal does the deciding where Burkhart here is concerned. You nor anybody else can step in for him." Claybourne moved a step backwards, toward the door. "Don't move, Burkhart, or I'll save the territory the cost of a trial!"

Jeff watched narrowly. He saw Claybourne halt at the doorway, turn his head slightly.

"Carl! Bill! Couple of you men come in here!" he yelled, directing his voice to the riders who apparently waited in the yard fronting the ranch house.

Jeff Burkhart waited no longer. His moments of freedom, of life itself, were slipping away with each receding second. He brought his arm around in a swift, sweeping motion. His fingers caught the album Cam Sutter had been glancing through, flung it straight at Claybourne.

He threw himself to one side as the foreman fired, careful this time not to trust his wounded leg too far. He came up under Claybourne's arms, drove the man hard into the door frame. Claybourne gasped with pain as the sharp corner of the wood came against his spine. His gun fell, *clattered* across the floor.

Burkhart smashed his fist into the man's face, saw him wilt, start to fall. He waited no longer. He leaped into the hallway, hearing as he did the slam of the front door.

"Straight ahead . . . that way!" Cam cried after him. "Leads to the back!"

Burkhart did not hesitate but threw open

111

the door at the end of the hall, plunged across the darkened room — a dining room, it appeared. Light was just ahead. A door with a glass panel. He jerked it open. He was on a screened-in porch. Beyond lay the yard with its scatter of buildings.

He was out into the open in a matter of moments. Behind him he could hear Abilene Dow's heavy voice shouting questions and the answers given by others as they searched through the house. He hurried along the length of the structure, favoring the injured leg that had begun to pain his considerably. He reached the corner of the building, turned.

The buckskin was somewhere ahead of him now. Another door slammed but he was away from the house, moving along a hedge of wild berry bushes. He came to its end, halted. He raised himself from a crouch, looked cautiously about. He spotted the buckskin twenty yards or so to his left. Taking a deep breath, he ran the remaining distance.

In the saddle, he threw a final glance at the ranch house. Shadows moved in the room where he had talked with Cam. Men were pouring into the front door and the regular slam of the kitchen screen marked their almost immediate exit on the far side.

Somewhere in the yard Abilene Dow was yelling.

"Get them horses! Hurry it up, damn it! Get some horses around here!"

A gun blasted through the confusion — unexpected, unexplained. Dow's voice roared its inquiry.

"Let go accidental-like, Ab! Nobody hurt!"

"Well, watch what you're doin'!" the gunman roared. "And nobody puts a gun on this joker we're huntin'. He's mine! Everybody understand that? Got a personal matter to settle with him!"

He swung away in the night, rode the buckskin hard for the first quarter hour, putting as much distance as possible between himself and Sutter's ranch. They would scour the country for him but he had a few minutes' start and with the darkness to shelter him he was not too worried; he could shake them.

But where could he go?

His leg, bleeding again, must be attended to. He ought to ride to his place, let Pete Langford doctor it for him — if Pete were still around. He could be in jail, put there by an angry Harry Wade. Even so, it would be dangerous to visit his own holdings. If the marshal had not already posted guards around it, Claybourne and his B-Bar-S men would be there, looking for him.

If he did not have the leg wound, he could hide out in the hills, in one of the thick groves. But it would be foolish to attempt that now. By morning his leg would be in such bad condition he would be fortunate to use it at all.

Where, then?

It came to him immediately. The place Harry Wade or Claybourne would be least likely to look for him would be the town itself. They would never guess he would choose Riflestock as a hiding place. At once he headed the tired little buckskin down the long plains that would take him into the settlement.

He could find a doctor there, too, get his leg looked after. And spend the rest of the night enjoying a little sleep and rest. He might even scare up a bite to eat. But he would have to be careful about being seen. Since his encounter with Animas and Searles, his face would be known.

It was a long, tiresome ride, and, when he entered the dark, deserted street, he was feeling light-headed. He located the doctor's residence, pounded on the door until he awakened him. He made known his needs, and the medic, a slight, gray man with a trailing mustache, conducted him to a back room where he cleaned and properly dressed the wound in strict silence.

Finished, Burkhart handed him two silver dollars. "Don't happen to have a room where a man could spend the rest of the night, do you?"

The doctor eyed him warily. "No, I wouldn't," he said, and led Burkhart back to the entrance.

"Any idea where I could find one?"

The physician, clearly unwilling to become involved in anything that might bring him trouble, pointed down the street with his chin. "Try the hotel. That's what they're in business for."

The hotel was, of course, out of the question. Burkhart did not think either Wade or Claybourne would look for him in Riflestock, but if they did, that place would likely be the very first they would visit. And he was taking no chances. "Besides that," he said.

"Only place I know," the medical man said, and closed the door.

Burkhart remained where he stood, on the narrow gallery fronting the physician's quarters, and studied the shadowed street. His leg felt much better; only the wearisome drag of twenty hours or so without sleep hammered at him with a dull insistence now. He glanced again toward the hotel, debating if it was worth the risk. He decided it was not. Stepping off the narrow porch, he walked to where the buckskin awaited him. He mounted to the saddle, pointed for the opposite corner where a sign proclaimed the location of the livery barn.

The hostler was asleep but the doors to the wide runway were open. Jeff swung down, moved its full length with the buckskin following at his heels. He located the rear entrance, and, after assuring himself of the exact position of all things, in event it became necessary to make a hasty departure, he sought out an empty stall. There he fed and watered his horse and bedded him down for the remainder of the night.

With his rifle in hand, he returned quietly to the front of the stable. The hostler still slept, undisturbed by the activity; thus assured, Burkhart sought out a place of rest for himself. A mound of straw near the back of the building offered the best possibilities and he sank down upon it gratefully.

He would have to be up and on his way before daylight, before the stableman and the town were up and about their business. That did not bother him. He would awaken in time. What did concern him was Cam

Sutter. He could not shake the feeling that, somehow, she was in danger. From whom or what, he was unsure. And he was satisfied Riley Claybourne knew more about Ben Sutter's murder than he was telling.

He wished he had been able to talk longer with Cam. He had not asked her all the questions he intended to. Claybourne's unexpected appearance at the house had prevented that. He still needed those answers. There was only one thing he could do. Go back to the ranch, see Cam Sutter again.

XV

Burkhart awakened in that pale, quiet hour before sunrise. He lay motionless for a long minute, getting his bearings, assuring himself he was alone. He got then to his feet. His leg at first was stiff, sore, but after a few experimental steps it loosened up and he gave it no more thought. Hunger, however, was a far different matter. He needed food. He had gone a full twenty-four hours now without eating and that, plus the loss of blood he had sustained from his wound, had weakened him. He must eat before he went much further.

He made his way to the front of the dark

117

and shadowy livery stable. The hostler still lay on his cot, snoring deeply. Jeff returned to the stall where he had left the buckskin. He saddled and bridled the little horse — now rested and ready for another hard day — and led him out into the runway. He chose the rear exit, preferring not to risk being seen by early risers of the town.

Once out of the barn, he stepped to the saddle and cut back along the rear of the buildings that stood shoulder to shoulder along Riflestock's one thoroughfare. The problem of food plagued him persistently and he knew that if he did not solve it now, while he was in the town, it would not be solved at all. And he would likely go another day without eating. That would be too dangerous, for just now Jeff Burkhart could not afford to drop from emptiness. He needed all his normal strength, and — if matters shaped up as he expected they would within the next twelve hours — all his talents and abilities.

The feeling that Cam Sutter was in danger again beset him and he could not shake it, nor could he determine in his own mind just where that danger lay. Morning's sober realization did clarify for him one thing. It had been a mistake to tip his hand to Claybourne — to let the man know he suspected him and his intentions. It could serve to force the foreman's hand, and, if that came to pass, Cam would be caught in the middle. There was no time to spare; he must get to her as soon as possible.

But for the present — his glance ran the far side of the street, found and halted upon the café. Smoke trickled upward from a stovepipe chimney and within the small building he could see a man moving about behind the counter.

Burkhart crossed over to the far line of buildings, started down an intersecting passageway — his plan was to come in behind the café and tie up the buckskin there where he would not be seen from the street. He rode the length of the narrow corridor, drew to a halt behind the café. There was no hitching rail and he tied the horse to a small tree that grew a few steps to one side. He made his way back to the street, keeping close to the wall of the café, threw his gaze to the far side. The porch before Hinton's was still empty. So, also, was the street. Burkhart breathed easier.

He turned then, entered the café. The owner glanced up. He had the dour, sullen face of a man who came to work early, went home late. Burkhart sat down at the brief counter, chose a stool far back from the

119

window.

"Coffee," he said. "What have you got that's ready?"

"Nothin' that's ready," the café man said gruffly. "Can give you eggs and bacon. Steak and potatoes take longer. You in a hurry?" He poured a cup of coffee from a blackened granite pot.

Burkhart took a deep swallow of the steaming liquid. He ignored the final question. "Make it bacon and eggs, double order. And leave that pot here where I can reach it."

The café man muttered something, shuffled off to his cooking quarters behind a makeshift partition. Jeff finished his first portion of coffee, poured himself a second. He was beginning to feel alive again. The sizzling of the frying food came to him and the delicious, tantalizing odor of the bacon filled his nostrils. Hunger began to rage through him, and to stifle it for another few minutes he helped himself to a doughnut from a round glass jar on the counter. It was stale and dry but he ate it with relish, washing it down with more coffee.

His platter of food, complete with warmed-up bread, arrived shortly after that. He ate rapidly, enjoyed each mouthful but fully conscious of the necessity for getting out of the town and on his way back to Sutter's ranch before any number of the town's citizens were abroad.

He was halfway through the eggs and bacon when he saw Abilene Dow. Dow and another man were riding into the far end of the street. Burkhart paused, watched the gunman and his companion travel the length of the dusty strip, their glances switching back and forth in the probing search of a bloodhound. It took no second thought to know they looked for him.

They halted before the doctor's residence where Jeff had sought attention for his leg. Dow dismounted, went to the door, and, without the formality of knocking, entered. Burkhart felt the café man's wondering stare upon him. He resumed his meal.

"Know that pair?"

Jeff said: "Maybe."

"Say," the café owner exclaimed, his eyes dropping to the short barreled Henry rifle lying on the counter near Burkhart's right hand, "ain't you the feller that killed them two out in the street a couple a days back? Claybourne's boys, they was."

Burkhart made no reply. He watched the front of the doctor's place closely, eating rapidly now. Two men came from the hotel, slanted across the street for the café. A

121

buckboard rolled up to Hinton's. A woman jumped lightly to the ground, crossed the porch, and disappeared inside.

Burkhart finished the last of the coffee in his cup. "How much I owe you?"

"Six bits. Ain't you that feller?"

Jeff laid a silver dollar on the counter, rose to his feet. The two men from the hotel reached the front entrance, halted there momentarily, arguing about something. Dow came from the medico's, mounted his horse. He glanced down the street, spoke to the cowboy with him. They separated, rode into opposing passageways, and were gone from view. Dow had not been outguessed. They were looking behind the buildings for his horse. He wished now he had taken time to conceal him better but it was too late to think about that now.

"Your change, mister," the café man said in a respectful voice.

"Keep it," Burkhart said. He reached into his pocket for another coin, suddenly remembering. Handing it to the man he said: "Appreciate your giving this to the hostler at the livery barn. Stabled my horse there last night. He was still sleeping when I left and I forgot to pay."

"Sure. Be right glad to."

The pair at the doorway concluded their

talk, entered, and sat down next to the window. Drummers, most likely.

Burkhart waited where he was — a tall, rigid shape in the center of the small room. He kept his eyes on the street. Dow would likely come to him from that point; it would be the rider with him who would spot the buckskin, return with the information. The gunman had chosen the buildings on the opposite side to check.

The drummers had ceased their jabbering. He felt their stares upon him, a vague interest in their eyes. He saw Dow return to the street, and a moment later the other B-Bar-S man. They conversed for a brief time, then, together, they started for the café, walking their horses slowly.

Burkhart tensed. He wanted no showdown with Dow at that moment; he did not have the time to spare. He should have gone when he saw them first enter the street. But most likely they would have seen him, anyway. Riflestock was of such size that a man leaving by any route would be noticed. He watched the pair draw nearer. If the gunman would have his try, then that was the way it would be. Dow would never rest until it was settled — Jeff realized that.

He saw Dow dismount, hitch at the gun slung low on his hip. The killer walked with deliberate slowness into the center of the lane, stopped. His hat was pushed to the back of his head, revealing a thatch of straw-colored hair. His face looked thinner, sharper.

"Burkhart!" he called. "I know you're in there. Come on out!"

Instantly the drummers slid from their seats, circled to the rear of the room, features alight with excitement.

"A gunfight, an honest-to-God gunfight," one of them breathed in a strained voice. "Always hearin' about one but never got to see it with my own eyes."

"Burkhart!"

Beyond the gunman Jeff saw Deputy Marshal Vic Antrum appear. And from the hotel near the lawman's office three more men came forth, all attracted by Dow's challenge. Burkhart's face clouded. Antrum's appearance altered the situation. With him present, and assuming he came out of the gun play with Dow, Jeff would face immediate arrest for the murder of Sutter. And locked in a jail cell he would be no help to Cam or anyone else.

"Is there a back door to this place?" he asked the café man.

"Yeah, sure."

"Burkhart! You don't come out, I'm

124

comin' in after you."

One of the drummers turned to Burkhart. "Ain't you goin' to fight him?" he asked in a plaintive voice. "He's callin' you out. Ain't you supposed to face him?"

Burkhart moved along the counter, backing all the way — never, for a single moment, taking his eyes off Abilene Dow and the other rider. He had no liking for what he was being compelled to do. Running away from anything was never a part of his make-up. But he had no other choice. He could afford no arrest, no confinement in a jail at this critical hour.

He reached the rear exit, paused with his fingers on the spool knob. "Keep your mouths shut," he said. "No point in any of you telling Dow I've gone. Let him find out for himself. Unless," he added, his voice dropping to a lower level, "you want trouble with me later."

The café man nodded his agreement quickly. The first drummer wagged his head. "You goin' to run? You ain't goin' out there and stand up to him?"

Burkhart favored the man with a dry grin. "Got business somewhere else. You do it for me," he said, and stepped into the open.

XVI

He headed directly for Sutter's B-Bar-S Ranch. He ignored the safety of the brushy hills in the interest of speed, and stayed to the main road. Pursuit by Abilene Dow — as well as by Deputy Antrum — would not be long in coming. And it placed him in a precarious situation. With them behind him and Marshal Harry Wade and his posse somewhere ahead, possibly scattered all through the Calaveras Hills and over its plains, he was rapidly getting himself pocketed. Add to that the very likely chance that Riley Claybourne with a party of his own was combing the land for him — and you came up with a not-too-promising answer as to Jeff Burkhart's chances.

But there was no turning back, not even if he had considered it. Too many important matters hung in the balance; too many problems were yet to be resolved. He had realized, at the beginning, that many difficulties faced him after his return to the Calaveras country — and he had undergone that baptism of violence. He was willing to step up and be counted when it came to settling scores. But he had not expected it to come so quickly. He scarcely had been afforded time enough to think.

He tried to visualize, as he rode steadily on, what Claybourne's next move would be. Dow's presence in Riflestock was easily explained. Claybourne had noted the injured leg, had assumed he would seek aid; since Burkhart was a stranger to the country, it was natural to assume he would hunt up the first doctor available. Acting on that hunch, Claybourne had sent the gunman into the town to investigate. Dow had probably asked for the chore, having built up in his mind an overpowering prejudice and a desire to redeem his fallen pride.

The fact that Claybourne had dispatched only Dow and one man to side him indicated to Jeff that he was conducting his own search. Likely he had paired up all the available men at B-Bar-S, had sent them poking into the hills and cañons and onto the plains in quest of Burkhart.

Was he with them or had he remained at the ranch where Cam was? That worried Burkhart considerably. Cam — alone, unprotected — would have no chance against a ruthless, ambitious man like Riley Claybourne if he had in mind to accomplish his purpose.

An hour out of Riflestock, Burkhart heard the steady, drumming hoof beats of a horse. They came not from behind him but ahead.

Immediately he swung off the road, drew up behind a dense stand of oak brush. Rifle laid across his legs, ready, he waited out the moments while the *thudding* sounds grew louder.

It was a buggy. He saw that first. It carried one passenger. A minute later he recognized Cam Sutter — her face a pale, drawn oval in the rising sunlight. Relief at once swept through him at seeing her safe, and he pulled out into the open to meet her. He saw her start in fear at his abrupt appearance, and then she recognized him. A cry of joy escaped her.

"Jeff!"

She stopped the buggy. He rode to its side, slipped from the saddle, and hurried to her. In another moment she had her arms about his neck.

"Oh, Jeff! I've been so afraid!"

He pulled away from her gently. "Claybourne?"

"I don't know," she murmured, her features still reflecting the terror that gripped her. "Somebody . . . out there in the brush . . . tried to shoot me!"

He knew then his fears had not been groundless. He held her tightly against his chest, trying to comfort her. He was standing in the road alongside the buggy. She had leaned forward off the seat.

"What happened after I left last night?" he asked, hoping to piece together some idea of a plan Riley Claybourne might be following.

"Riley was like a wild man. He called in Dow and all the others that were on the ranch. They searched the house for you, and, when they didn't find anything, they went outside and hunted some more. Some of them rode off while others just kept on looking around the ranch. I never before saw Riley like he was last night. Oh, he's always been stern and hard and all business but last night he was like a crazy man . . . someone I didn't even know." She paused. "Didn't you run into any of the crew? They went everywhere."

He said: "Saw Dow in town. Claybourne must have figured I'd go and get my leg doctored."

She looked at him intently. "Did . . . did you have to shoot him?"

He shook his head. "Left before it got down to that. Couldn't spare the time. But it will come, sooner or later. Dow won't let it die. Last night, did Claybourne ride out with the others?"

"I don't know if he went with them, but he did leave. I remember suddenly realizing

129

I was there alone. I got dressed and went out to the barn, feeling that I couldn't stand it there by myself. I hitched up the buggy and started for town. Not long after that I saw . . . or maybe heard . . . somebody riding off to one side, deep in the brush. Then the shot came."

Her flow of words ceased. She glanced fearfully about at the slowly lightening hills. She trembled violently against him.

"Who would want to kill me, Jeff?"

"I don't know," he answered, "but I've a mighty strong hunch. Did Claybourne ever ask you to marry him?"

Her eyes swung to him, startled. A frown crinkled her brow. "Why, yes, he did. A week or two ago. I told him I wasn't interested, of course. What's that got to do with all this?"

"It could have a lot to do with it," he said flatly.

"You mean you think Riley is the one who tried to shoot me . . . who killed my father?"

"Looks like the best bet to me."

"Why? Why would he want to do it?"

"Stop and think. Your father's ranch is practically his. He's been running it just like it was his own, the way it suited him. He even hired gunfighters to back his play. The only thing wrong with it all was that he actually didn't own it. What was the answer

130

to that? Why, get rid of your father, of course. That made you sole heir and owner. Then, if possible, marry you. The ranch would thus be his. If you weren't interested in his offer, it wouldn't create too great a problem. He would simply get you out of the way. That could account for the shot somebody took at you this morning. And, if it had hit its mark, who would have been saddled with blame?"

"You!"

"Of course. He has already hung the murder of your father around my neck . . . convinced the marshal and everybody else who will listen that I did it because of a grudge. It would be natural for me to finish off the last of the Sutter family, wouldn't it? I would have had a hard time proving my innocence but he wasn't even taking a chance on that. He was trying to fix it so I would never get to trial. He or some of his gunslicks were planning to hunt me down and finish me off before time. As posse members running down a killer they had good reason to shoot first and talk later."

Cam shuddered. "Riley Claybourne," she murmured in a lost sort of voice. "It's hard to believe. But it makes sense now. Only thing, this proposal of his . . . that was maybe two weeks ago, not just yesterday."

Jeff shrugged. "Doesn't matter. He has probably had the plan in mind for some time. That could have been just a build up. Something to make it look good. If he asked you to marry him now, it would look like he was doing it only because your father was dead and you are alone. As it was, you would be remembering that he made a proposal long before it happened and think he wanted you for yourself and not for what was yours."

She was silent a long minute. "What do we do now, Jeff? Where can we go?"

"Wade's posse is probably scattered all around us," he said thoughtfully. "And I'm expecting Dow and maybe Antrum to come up this road from town 'most any minute."

"Would we be safe at the ranch?"

He considered that. "Yes," he said. "That's the best bet. If we have to, we can fort up there. Either Wade or Antrum will eventually show up, and I'll have my chance to make them listen to me."

Cam glanced back up the road, along the route she had just covered. "I'm almost afraid to drive. . . ."

"We won't use the buggy," he said. "We'll pull it off the road, hide it. You can ride my horse. I'll unhitch yours and use him. That way we can keep to the brush, out of sight."

A tremor passed through her again. "Oh, Jeff, if you hadn't come along when you did. . . ."

"I had a feeling all the time I should get back to you," he said. "And I always follow my hunches."

He reached out to take her in his hands, swing her down from the seat. She held back momentarily, threw her arms about his neck, and kissed him once again.

"Jeff, I never knew it was possible to care so much. . . ."

"We've got a whole lifetime ahead of us for it," he added.

They were paused there like that, in each others arms, when the bullet came shrilling out of the brush for her. It clipped through the sleeve of her light jacket, smashed into the seat's backrest, splintered it. The echo of the blast rolled through the choppy hills in a slowly fading repetition of sound.

XVII

Jeff Burkhart's military training and experience reacted for him. Without conscious thought, he seized the girl about the waist, swung her away from the buggy. They went prone to the ground. He did not stop there. He grabbed her wrist, came to his knees, and crawled rapidly for the nearest sheltering brush, half dragging her in his wake.

It had taken only seconds to reach safety. They crouched there behind the scrubby oak growth and listened. They would not be safe for long, Burkhart knew. Their concealment was only temporary. They must find better, more substantial cover. The hidden marksman would soon locate the brush behind which they had hidden, riddle it with bullets. And thin oak leaves would offer no resistance to leaden slugs.

He glanced cautiously about, taking care to keep low. The ambusher had not seen the exact point where they had taken refuge, otherwise he would have opened up with his gun again. If they could move once more, before he discovered them, they would have a chance for escape.

Ahead, a dozen steps, he saw a large boulder. Brushy growth covered the ground surrounding it. He pressed Cam's hand.

"We can't stay here. Got to get to that rock up ahead. Follow close behind me . . . and stay low."

She said: "All right, Jeff."

Flat on his belly, he crawled from the tangle of oak, his eyes probing ceaselessly the slopes and brush ahead and to either side. It was so thick at this point he could see nothing, detect no movement that revealed the location of the sniper. But he was there, hidden somewhere, awaiting his chance to kill.

They gained the shelter of the rock, huddled up behind it. Burkhart checked his rifle, levered it softly, part way, to assure himself a cartridge was in the chamber. He carefully examined the end of the barrel for dirt accidentally pushed into the opening while he crawled. It was clean. The Henry was ready.

Jeff glanced around, now dissatisfied with their position.

"No good waiting here," he murmured. "Like rabbits waiting to get pot shot. I'm going out and get that sniper."

At once Cam laid her hands on his arm, stayed him. "Wouldn't it be better to just wait?"

"I don't think so. He could work around, get us in his sights from the side, without us ever knowing it. Better I flush him out before he can do that."

She leaned forward, kissed him. "Be careful, Jeff, for my sake."

"I'll be back," he said. "Don't move. Stay here behind this rock."

She nodded, watched as he flattened himself to the ground, began to worm his way to another, similar pile of stones a few yards farther up the slope. The wild grass and ground brush was well over knee high and he had no difficulty in keeping below the vision of anyone watching the hillside.

It was like the old days in the Army, Jeff thought. Times when he — with the short-barreled Henry, ideal for such an operation — made his way through grass and weeds to look upon the enemy quartered in a nearby valley, or perhaps to ferret out a hidden gun emplacement that was holding back Sheridan's advance.

He had made numberless such excursions, always feeling the tense thrill of the moments, always glorying in the fact that he could accomplish such a mission, which to many others was a near impossibility. This time it was different. There was no thrill, no exultation in what he had taken on. Today the life of the girl he loved depended upon his abilities, his talent to move, unseen and unheard, along the slope of the low-crowned hill. If he failed, they both would die.

He crawled in behind the mass of stones and brush, breathing heavily from his efforts. He was softer than he had thought, then he remembered the wound in his leg. It could be slowing him down some, making it harder to move. He lay quietly for a time, listening. He heard nothing and, moving to one side, threw his glance upwards. A longer stretch of open ground lay between him and the next sheltering cover, this time a thickly growing stand of wild berry bushes. He would have to be at his best to gain that point unseen by the sniper.

He froze, hearing a sound behind him. He twisted swiftly, silently, his rifle coming up in a quick blur. It was Cam Sutter. He felt a mixture of anger and alarm rise within him as she crawled, with painful slowness, through the undergrowth.

But she made it without incident, pulled herself in beside him, breathless and tired.

"You shouldn't have tried that!" he scolded sharply. "You might have been seen."

She glanced up to him, her eyes pure green now in the bright sunlight. "I couldn't stay there, Jeff. I want to be with you, no matter what happens."

He shook his head, seemingly finding that hard to comprehend. He pointed to the cluster of berry bushes. "It's long way to the next stop. You'll have to stay put this time."

"If you can chance it, I can, too."

"Chance is just what it is . . . and a big one. If I just had some idea where that

137

bushwhacker was hiding." He glanced at her yellow scarf, an idea coming to him. "Let me borrow that for a minute."

She removed it at once, handed it to him. He picked up a stone the size of his fist, wrapped the square of silk about it, and tied it securely with its corners.

"Maybe this will draw him out," Burkhart said, and threw the rock with its bright covering fifty yards or so up the slope.

Instantly the hills echoed with the sound of a shot. Jeff saw dust leap upward where the bullet struck, only inches from the bright splash of color. He saw, also, the faint puff of smoke that marked the position of the sniper.

"Now," he said with deep satisfaction, "we know what we're doing." He studied the slope to their right. "If I can cross over, I'll be directly below him. With a little luck I can circle and come in from behind. Then Little Henry here can go to work," he added, patting the short-barreled rifle confidently.

"With a little luck," Cam repeated.

"Like I said, we just can't sit here and wait for him to. . . ."

"I know," she broke in, "but I'm afraid you might be seen, or get caught in a trap of some kind. There could be more than

138

one of them."

"I don't think so. But don't worry about it. Nothing will happen to me. I'll be across that strip and in behind that scrub oak before our bushwhacker friend knows what's up."

"And from there?"

"Depends on what's farther on. Bound to be rocks and more bushes. There will be something I can hide behind."

"I'm going, too," she said suddenly.

He faced her, his features stern. "Not this time. Too much in the open, out there. I want you to stay right here, in this exact spot. I mean it! And I want your promise you will do it, Cam."

She saw the worry in his eyes. "All right," she said after a moment. "I won't follow. I promise."

"Good," he answered, relieved. "Both of us crawling around on that slope might draw attention. By myself I'll have no trouble. I want you to remain right where you are, then I'll know where to find you."

He crawled out onto the slope immediately after that, began to make his way toward the clump of oak. The grass and weed growth was thinner here and he knew he was not so well covered as he had been farther down the hillside. But he kept low, aware he was beneath the tops of the spare stalks.

He halted when near halfway to get his directions. He removed his hat, lifted his head cautiously. Only a few more feet to the brush. He dropped flat again, continued on. When he paused that next time, he was under the scalloped leaves of the scrubby growth.

He rolled over on his back, looked toward Cam. She still crouched behind the rocks, her face turned toward him. He raised himself to a sitting position, waved to her that all was well. He saw her smile, lift her hand in acknowledgement.

He pulled himself deeper into the scrub oak. Directly before him the slope grew steeper with no cover at all on its surface except a thin scatter of grass and weeds. At the far edge of that, perhaps fifty yards, stood a small grove of trees. The ambusher, unless Burkhart guessed wrong, had stationed himself within it.

To Jeff's right the slope dipped into a deep arroyo, well filled with loose rock, dry leaves, dead tree limbs, and other bits of forest litter washed into it by rains. To attempt a climb up its narrow course, unheard or unseen, was an impossibility. Beyond it, however, prospects were better. A low ridge of rocks ran along its edge, a formation not unlike a wall. If he could get to that, he would have no problem making his way to the grove and slipping in behind the sniper.

He turned his attention back to the grove, to that section where he had seen the telltale puff of smoke. Apparently the hidden rifleman had immediately discovered the scarf had been only a trick and was not one of his intended victims. He had not pursued the matter further, had instead remained in hiding. Jeff had hoped it would bring him out into the open, but in that it had failed. It had succeeded in pointing out his approximate location — and that was of great help.

He set himself to picking a route to the wall of rock. He saw at once he was faced with a decision — should he simply get to his feet, race across the short distance, gambling on the marksmanship of the sniper, or should he stay low, as he had been doing, and continue to crawl? The latter would be difficult to accomplish. At the edge of the ravine the grass ended. From there to the rocks, a distance of twenty-five feet or more, he would be in the open, fully exposed.

He swung his attention down the slope, considered the advisability of dropping

141

back, circling lower, and approaching from the far side of the arroyo. It would involve too much time, and cover was little better in that area. There would be no advantage in such a move.

He thought then of employing the old trick of providing his own concealment, cutting a thick cluster of brush, holding it over his body like an umbrella while he crawled the distance. He discarded that idea, also. Such a ruse worked where there was some masking growth in which to move. It was useless under conditions he now faced.

He decided to make a run for it. For one thing it would draw the rifleman's attention to him, away from where Cam was hiding. And, when he sprang out to use his gun, he would immediately reveal his exact position. That would afford Burkhart a chance to bring his own rifle into action.

He got to his knees, remained that way while he breathed deeply, getting himself set for the sprint. He glanced over his shoulder to Cam. She was watching him closely, her features serious, her eyes appearing large in the oval frame of her face. She had drawn herself up closer to the butte of rocks, either as a means for seeing him better or making herself more completely hidden.

He took a firm grip on the Henry rifle, came to a crouch. He lunged away from the oak brush, started for the ravine and its ridge of stone, his long legs reaching out to full stride. He was aware instantly of a burst of smoke, a faint flash of orange off to his left. Something akin to a thunderbolt smashed into his arm, high up, near the shoulder. He was conscious of being spun swiftly about. A loud report filled his ears.

Suddenly he was on his back, looking up into a sky that wheeled dizzily overhead.

XVIII

As if from some vast distance Jeff heard Cam Sutter screaming. He tried to pull himself up, reach a sitting position. Strangely he had no strength. The entire left side of his body was numb, seemingly no part of his regular self.

He twisted his head, looked toward the rocks, to the girl. A wave of horror swept through him when he saw her coming, running on all fours like a slim, fleet antelope.

"Stay back!" he croaked hoarsely. "Don't try to come here!"

She reached him, unharmed, crouched down beside him even before he had finished his words. She was crying and he

143

regarded her with frowning wonder.

"Jeff! Jeff!"

The frantic calling of his name slowly penetrated the fog that locked in his brain. He shook his head, tried to sit up. She pressed him back and he struggled against her.

"No . . . help me! Got to get up!"

Some deep-seated instinct was pushing at him, insisting that he rise. For what cause his clouded mind was not aware at that exact moment; his subconscious self knew only that danger was nearby, that he must prepare himself to meet it.

He fought to rise. She helped him, her worried eyes on the wound in his shoulder. His brain, at last, began to clear as pain started a steady, throbbing trail through his body. He stared at Cam Sutter, at the thick clump of oak behind which they hid, at the sloping hillsides and shallow ravines and high, blue sky all about them. And suddenly he was conscious of the moment, of their peril.

He twisted about, managed to get to his knees. The effort sent a shocking wave of pain through him but he ignored it as best he could. He listened into the morning quiet. Only moments had passed since the bullet had felled him; the killer should be moving in for the final blow. He heard the faint rattle of brush, the dry slipping of disturbed gravel. Somewhere above them on the slope — between the oak thicket where they crouched and the grove.

The bushwhacker, not certain his shot had been a fatal one, was approaching cautiously to see, to complete his job. He would find Cam, would have them both.

"Get behind me," he said in a low whisper.

His left arm hung limply at his side, of no use to him. Cam had wrapped something about it, stanching the flow of blood. He waited there on his knees while she crawled around to a position at his back.

Jeff checked his rifle. He could not recall if he had fired it or not. The moments prior to his taking the bullet in his shoulder were hazy, incomplete in his memory. There was a cartridge in the chamber. The Henry was ready.

He felt Cam against him. Her body, touching his lightly, trembled. He wished he could comfort her, put his arm about her and assure her that everything would come out all right. But he had only one arm and in it he held his weapon.

He heard then the distant, oncoming *thud* of running horses. The sound was to the north, in the direction of Sutter's ranch —

not from Riflestock. That was some relief; at least it was not Abilene Dow, arriving on the scene to press his desire for a showdown. It was probably Marshal Harry Wade and some of his posse, attracted by the gunshots.

There was a sudden *clatter* of brush over to their right, near the ravine where the wall of rock stood. He swiveled his attention to that point sharply. The bushwhacker had apparently changed his course of approach, had moved farther over seeking the protection of the ridge. Jeff raised himself slightly, threw a glance to that point.

He saw the dark, crouched shape of a man edging toward them through the brush. He brought the Henry to his shoulder, waited out the terrible moments for a clear shot. The threatening figure stepped into the open, rifle snapping quickly into position when he saw Cam and Jeff only a few paces away. Burkhart's jaw sagged in surprise.

Pete Langford!

Jeff stared, not immediately understanding what he looked upon. Langford came to a weaving halt. His face was contorted, worked spasmodically. His eyes blazed with an insane light.

"Pete! What are you doing here . . . ?"

"Get out of my way, boy! Don't concern you none! It's them thievin' damn' Sutters

I'm after. . . ."

Burkhart saw Langford level his long-barreled rifle at a target beyond him, realized instantly the target was Cam. "No, Pete!" he yelled. "No!"

He saw it was hopeless, of no use to try and stop the old man. He fired the Henry, taking no time to aim, only to keep the crazed man from pulling the trigger of his own weapon.

The impact of the bullet staggered Langford. He went backwards a short step. Reflex action set off the rifle he held but the muzzle was pointed upward and the bullet went singing off into the sky. He dropped the gun, sank to his knees, and slowly wilted.

Jeff Burkhart got to his feet, ran to where the old man lay. Cam was with him and he was aware also of riders pounding up and sliding to a halt. He knelt down beside Langford, rolled him over gently onto his back.

"Pete, I'm sorry I had to. . . ."

Langford opened his eyes. He looked much older, lying there. His features seemed sharper, the bones of his face more pronounced. His gray hair was thinner, only wisps.

"It's all right, boy," he said. "Reckon I'm sorry about shootin' you. You hadn't ought

147

to have jumped up like that. But I ain't sorry about Ben Sutter . . . and I wouldn't 'a' been sorry for that girl of his'n, either."

Jeff heard Cam crying softly at his elbow. He glanced to the right. Marshal Harry Wade stood by, listening closely. Beyond him were several others, one of whom was the deputy, Vic Antrum.

Wade moved up closer. "Pete, you say you killed Ben Sutter?"

Langford nodded weakly. "I sure did. And I would have finished up the job if the boy here hadn't messed up things."

"You about got him hung for it," Wade said.

Langford frowned. "Things is sort of mixed up in my head. Them Sutters euchred me out of my place and everybody started blamin' Jeff when I took it on to get even. Can't say as I rightly know what happened but I wouldn't have let you harm the boy."

Wade shrugged. "You cut it mighty close. My men had orders to shoot on sight. Either we took him alive and hung him or we killed him out here in the hills."

Langford's eyes were clouding. The muscles of his face were going slack. "Reckon . . . things just sort of . . . got out of hand. . . ."

Jeff Burkhart rose to his feet slowly. His

arm pained him steadily and there was a lightness in his head. Cam took him by the wrist.

"Come over here and sit down. In the shade. I've got to fix that bandage. Then we're going to town and see the doctor."

Burkhart did not move. He faced Wade. "You satisfied, Marshal?"

The lawman said: "I'm satisfied. Sorry I put you through what I did. But that's the way the chips fall sometimes. Evidence don't always point in the right way."

Burkhart turned from him, threw his glance to the other men grouped beyond the marshal. He was looking for Riley Claybourne. He had been wrong about the foreman, at least where Ben Sutter's death was concerned. He owed the man an apology for that, if for nothing else. But the big foreman was not present.

Cam said: "Your shoulder, Jeff. Let me fix it. Then we'll get to the buggy and go to town."

He followed her obediently to the clump of scrub oak. He sat down and she began to tend the wound, binding it with a bandage improvised from the lower border of her petticoat. While she worked, he watched Wade and the others load Pete Langford's lifeless body onto a horse and ride off

149

toward Riflestock.

"Did . . . did my father cheat him?" Cam asked in a small voice.

"I don't think so," Jeff replied. "Pete told me he was paid for his land as well as the stock he had on it. Maybe Claybourne sort of prodded him into making the deal, but I think it was a fair one. Something else got to working in his mind. A kind of a poison, I guess you would call it."

"A poison?"

"You know what I mean. He just got to thinking about it and turned sorry that he sold out. Somehow he started blaming your father for his own mistake and that kept chewing at him until it became something big . . . and plenty bad. It finally included everything and anything that was connected with the Sutters."

"The poor man," Cam murmured. "I think my father would have given his place back to him, if he had known it was that way."

"If he had known," Jeff echoed, thinking then of Riley Claybourne.

They started down the slope at a slow walk. Jeff no longer felt dizzy and light-headed. It was simply a deep weariness now, a long tiredness that dragged at his muscles and stiffened his frame. It would be good to lie down, to sleep for days.

They reached the road, crossed over. "We'll tie your horse on behind," she said, looking about for the vehicle and the two animals.

"Stable him when we get to town," he said. "When the doc's finished with me, I'm going into that hotel and sleep for a spell."

"Not at the hotel," she corrected. "At the ranch."

Burkhart sighed. It would be good to get onto the seat of the buggy, just to sit and relax. And then he saw they were not alone, that there was someone with the buggy.

Abilene Dow.

XIX

Jeff Burkhart came to a stop. He heard a small gasp of surprise, of fear, come from Cam's lips. He took three slow and careful steps to one side, pulled away from her.

"Been waitin' for you," Dow said in a toneless voice.

"So I see," Burkhart murmured. His mind was clear now. All the hazy fog was gone, the light-headedness. His shoulder still pained dully but it was of no importance, not at this moment.

Over the brief distance that separated

them, Burkhart asked: "You sure you want this? I've got no quarrel with you. It's all in your head."

"I want it," Dow replied. "Carl Animas was a friend of mine. So was Searles. And I got me another friend, too."

There was movement over to Dow's left. Burkhart saw Riley Claybourne glide into view from behind a thick tree. The big foreman halted, said nothing, merely watched.

All Burkhart's thought concerning Claybourne clarified into truth suddenly. The foreman had been working and planning to take over Sutter's B-Bar-S, just as he had suspected. Likely he had plotted Ben Sutter's death, too — only Langford had stepped in and relieved him of that necessity. Jeff realized he had almost become the perfect patsy.

He glanced at Claybourne, standing to one side like a tall, dark-featured vulture, waiting only to claim the spoils. If he failed, if Dow cut him down, Claybourne would have the ranch — and Cam, too.

Abilene Dow was the key. To the gunman he said: "Appears he's more than a friend. Your boss, too."

"Could be you're right."

"Must have put a bit of starch in your knees. I remember your ducking back

152

through a saloon a couple of days back."

"I recollect you did some runnin' yourself, early this mornin'."

"Not because I was afraid of you, Dow. But of your friend here and what he might do. I didn't have the time to waste."

"You got it now, mister!"

Cam Sutter cried out, threw herself in front of Jeff. "No . . . he's been hurt! Can't you see that? You can't fight him. I won't let you!"

"He's got one good arm, lady," Dow said. "That's all he needs."

Again Burkhart moved away from the girl. Without taking his eyes off Dow, he said: "I'll be all right. Don't worry."

"But you are so weak! You're in no condition to do this."

"Take only a minute," he said, his words low. "Stand over to one side, out of the way. If anything goes wrong, get to one of the horses and try to catch up with Wade and the others. They'll be somewhere between us and town."

She nodded woodenly, walked slowly away.

"Where do you stand in this?" Burkhart asked, directing his question at Claybourne. "Do I put my second bullet in you?"

The foreman shrugged.

"If I go down, then the road's clear and you take over. I don't and it turns out the other way, you just happened to be here watching, that it?"

"Could be," Riley Claybourne said.

"You talk mighty big," Dow broke in. "Sounds like you maybe figure to walk away from this."

"I will," Burkhart said in a flat, cold voice. "You haven't got a chance."

A flicker of apprehension crossed Abilene Dow's thin features. He licked at his lips, moved slightly on his feet.

"All right. Any time you feel like dying," Jeff Burkhart said softly.

"Damn you!" Dow yelled, and clawed for the weapon at his hip.

The Henry rifle pivoted upward in Jeff Burkhart's hand. There was the double blast of both guns, fired at an identical fragment of time. Jeff felt the Henry jump under the grasp of his fingers. A numbing shock raced up his arm. Dow's bullet had struck the rifle somewhere. He did not glance away to see. He watched the gunman and in the same instant brought the muzzle of his rifle to bear on Riley Claybourne.

Dow stood motionlessly, arms hanging loosely at his sides, gun pointed downward. His face bore a startled, wondering expression, as if something had just taken place that he could not fully comprehend. His lips began to move, to form words.

"I ain't about to. . . ."

The stammering ceased abruptly. The gun dropped from his hand, and he fell forward upon it.

Burkhart's gaze was on Claybourne. The big foreman stood silently off to one side, his arms held well away from his body. If it had been his intention to draw and fire at Burkhart immediately when he saw that Dow had failed, he had waited too long.

"How about it, Riley?"

Claybourne stared at him for a long moment. Then he moved his head back and forth gently. "No," he said, "price is too high." And turning, he walked to where his horse stood.

Burkhart watched the man in silence, never taking his rifle off him. He waited until Claybourne was near, cutting across before him, striking for the road.

"This country's not for you," he said.

Claybourne looked at him intently, nodded. "Agreed," he murmured, and continued on.

Jeff heard Cam cry out her relief and joy, and all at once she was before him, her arms about him as she sobbed her happiness.

With his good arm he held her close while the tension of the past moments slowly ebbed from his body.

He glanced at the rifle in his hand, wondering then where Dow's bullet had scored. He saw at once; near the muzzle, in that small space that separated the barrel from its tubular magazine. The gun was damaged beyond repair and further use. It was fortunate that Riley Claybourne had not noticed.

"Guess that's the finish of Little Henry," he said, thinking aloud.

Cam stepped back from him, dropped her eyes to the rifle. She saw the twisted magazine, the dented, crooked barrel. She shuddered. "His bullet didn't miss you by far."

"Like losing on old friend," Burkhart murmured. "A real good friend."

She studied his features for a time. Then: "Even friends some day die."

He nodded. "And it's never an easy thing to accept."

She laughed, took the rifle from his hands. "Well, maybe this friend won't be doing any more fighting, but at least he'll be around where we can see him."

Burkhart looked at the girl in astonishment. "What are you . . . ?"

"There will be a couple of pegs over our fireplace where we'll hang Little Henry.

156

Then we can look at him and remember."

He understood at that moment. "Remember that it was Little Henry who made it possible for us to stay together, that it?"

"That's it," she said. Taking him by the arm, she started toward the buggy.

RANGE FEUD

I

Jess Holloway first noticed the dust cloud when he broke out of a dense grove of scrub cedar and started down a slope that led into a brush-choked arroyo. The yellowish pall was neither large nor particularly heavy; it appeared to be moving steadily along the mesa that lay above and beyond a wall of ragged, red-colored buttes that faced him from the far end of the sandy wash. It could be cattle — but that explanation somehow failed to satisfy him; a rancher drifting stock to better range would not be pushing them so hard.

But it had been a dry spring, he reckoned, allowing his glance to probe the rolling country, and the soil was powdery, easily stirred. Ranchers would be finding it hard going with the springs dried up and the rivers low. Few things affected cattle raising so vitally as did the lack of water.

He guessed that was one of the reasons

Saul Morrel's widow had written him to come; Saul had died, or had been killed — he wasn't sure which — and she had turned to him for help.

He had quit a good foreman's job in Texas to answer the summons, but that didn't bother him — he had been fiddle-footed all his life — he hoped only that he could fulfill the confidence Marie Morrel apparently placed in him. Saul had been like a father during the years they had worked together and he had long sought for a means to show his appreciation. Now, finally, it had come.

He looked again at the dust cloud. It had grown, was much nearer, and seemed to be moving directly for the rim of the bluffs towering a hundred feet or so above the floor of the arroyo. Holloway frowned, studied the trail ahead. It did not end at the arroyo's termination, he saw, but continued on, climbing the buttes through a narrow gash that would eventually bring him out on the top. Satisfied, he settled back. Once on the rim he could satisfy his curiosity.

He wondered about Marie Morrel, what sort of woman she was. Her letter had been brief, almost curt, and she hadn't mentioned a son. There had been one — Saul had spoken of him a few times. His name was Dave and at that time he was living with his

162

mother in the East. Saul was working to build a stake and start a ranch of his own. He planned to send for them then.

That time had come six, or perhaps it was seven years ago. Together they were working for the A-Bar spread in Arizona when one spring morning Morrel had turned to Jess and said simply: "I'm quitting. Got enough cash now to start ranching."

Holloway had stared at him in amazement, surprised by the suddenness of it all. But that was the way Saul Morrel did things. "Glad to hear it," he said.

"Been a fine thing, knowing you. If you're ever needing a job, ride over to my place."

"Your place?" Jess had echoed. "Knew you were figuring on one . . . didn't know you already had it."

"Got a house, barn, about two hundred head of stock . . . not much else. Cimarron country of New Mexico."

"But you've not been gone. How . . . ?"

"Had a couple of fellows getting things ready. Been at it quite a spell. Word come yesterday it was all set."

Jess had stepped forward, shaken Saul Morrel's hand. "Obliged to you for the offer . . . I'll sure remember it. And I'm turning it right around . . . you ever need me, just holler."

163

That had been the last he had heard or seen of Morrel until he received the letter — a letter that had followed him from Arizona, to New Mexico, and finally to Texas. It was two months old when he opened it. Immediately he had dispatched a reply advising Saul's widow that he was on his way, and two days later he was in the saddle.

The Slash M was the Morrel spread, the letter had told him. There were no other details except that he would find the ranch in New Mexico Territory, south of the Cimarron River. He had been through that part of the country once or twice, recalled now that it was a lush, grassy lowland, broken occasionally by tall buttes and arroyos floored with white sand.

He had camped one night in a grove of cottonwoods near the Cimarron, building a fire of greasewood and creosote bush, and later lain there, staring up into a diamond-studded velvet sky while coyotes sang in the distance. It had been a night to remember.

But for all its beauty it had then been a troubled country, one where violence rode the hills and mesas as a hard-eyed man known as Clay Allison led a band of small ranchers in rebellion against a powerful land syndicate. He wondered if the matter was still unresolved, if Marie Morrel's need for him had anything to do with the Allison-syndicate war.

He hoped not. He'd had his time fighting range battles and had vowed never to get himself involved again in such a cause. Usually they solved nothing — left only festering sores that sooner or latter had to be faced. But if the Morrel problem proved to be of that nature, he would do what was asked of him; he owed it to Saul Morrel.

The arroyo began to narrow, turn shallow. He looked beyond the ears of his roan horse; they were nearing the butte with the gash that permitted ascent to the crest.

Holloway threw a final glance to the sky above the rim. He was too close now to see the dust cloud, but it had been there only moments before — a low boil floating steadily toward the edge of the buttes.

Abruptly gunshots cracked hollowly through the hot air. Jess paused, reached down to rub the roan's sweaty neck while he listened. A tall, lean, dark-haired man well into his twenties, he had deep-set eyes and a thin line for a mouth that gave him a look of firm resolve.

Faint yells reached him, the continuing racket of gunshots, and a low, drumming sound. Brushing at the beads on his face,

165

he touched the gelding with spurs and urged him up the trail.

He topped out through a patch of feathery Apache plume and glanced ahead. The dust cloud lay a quarter mile or less in front of him, hovered now above a fall in the land. The shooting and yells were below it.

At that moment a small jag of steers, two dozen or so, bobbed suddenly into view over the lip of the swale and raced toward him — and the edge of the butte. Two riders came into sight, holding close on the heels of the stock, urging them on with shouts and gunshots.

Amazement, and then anger, surged through Jess Holloway as realization came to him; the two men were deliberately driving the cattle to their deaths over the rim of the butte.

Waiting no longer, he fumbled in his saddlebags for a bit of cloth, came up with an old undershirt, and then, drawing his six-gun, charged straight at the oncoming herd.

II

Holloway, waving the shirt before him and firing his pistol, saw the lead steers slow uncertainly. Immediately the two riders began to yell louder, renewed their efforts to keep the cattle running — straight for Jess and the cliff behind him.

Again anger rushed through Holloway. He twisted half about, snapped a shot at the nearest cowpuncher, dimly visible through the dust. The man veered off, unhurt but visibly startled. His hat fell, and Jess had a glimpse of thick, red hair.

A bullet *clicked* against his saddle horn, screamed off into space. Instantly he fired a reply at the second rider — older, darker than the first. He did not flinch and pull away, but calmly leveled his weapon for another try at Jess.

Holloway wheeled then, rode directly into the thick, swirling dust, offering the man no target. The herd was swinging aside now, beginning to run parallel with the rim of the butte. Emerging abruptly from the pall, Jess had another quick look at the redhead, bending low from his horse recovering his hat. He jerked himself upright abruptly as Holloway's bullet spurted sand in his face and, jamming spurs to his horse, spun away.

Pistol empty, Jess kept the blue roan moving while he punched out the empty cartridges and reloaded. Ready again, he cut back into the dust, slowed when he saw the two outlaws moving toward him.

He grinned tightly. The pair didn't like his horning in on their little game of slaughter and breaking it up; now they were concentrating on him. He leveled on the dark man, squeezed off a shot. The rider flinched, halted abruptly and clutched at his arm. The redhead gave him a hurried glance, and then both men wheeled and lined out for the distant hills at a hard gallop.

Holloway flung two more shots at them, and settled back on his saddle again to replace the spent bullets in his weapon. Evidently the redhead and his dark friend had no taste for a head-on clash.

He looked toward the cattle. The herd had halted in a small hollow a short distance away and were beginning to settle down and graze on the short grass. Putting the roan into motion, he rode toward the swale. Halfway there, he halted. Two more riders were approaching, coming in from the north.

Holloway studied them for several moments, then continued on. Reaching the dust-covered steers, he once again stopped and took note of the brand: Box K. Not any of Morrel's stock, he saw, and felt a curious relief at the discovery. Lifting his glance, he watched the newcomers draw close. His pistol was still in his hand, and, shifting his weight, he slid it back into its holster, but he was still cautious. These could be Box K cowpunchers searching for the cattle — or they could be friends of the redhead and more trouble.

Both were middle-aged, and one a Mexican dressed in *vaquero* clothing. He grinned broadly as they circled the herd and drew up in front of Holloway.

"Muchas gracias, amigo," he said, brushing his ornamented hat to the back of his head. "If you had not come this way, we would have some very dead cows."

The other cowpuncher nodded. "Pete's right, mister. Sure obliged to you. . . ." He stared off into the direction the outlaws had taken. "Sure tricked us. . . ."

"Who are they?" Holloway asked, easing back on the saddle.

"One of them's called Nemo . . . the other's Red. Ain't never heard no other names." The cowpuncher paused, motioned to the Mexican. "Partner here's Pete Gonzales. I'm Ed Floyd."

Jess nodded. "Holloway, Jess Holloway. Pleased to know you. That stock yours?"

"Belongs to Tom Lindsey . . . Box K. We ride for him. Pete and me was drifting them over to the south range. We seen some jasper fooling around another bunch of steers west of here. We rode over to see what the hell was going on . . . there's been some rustling lately . . . and soon's we was out of sight, Red and Nemo must've jumped in behind and stampeded our cattle toward the cliff. Where was you?"

Jess waved at the arroyo below the butte. "Just happened to be riding this way. Saw the dust and heard shooting. When I got to the top, I ran smack into the herd."

"Mighty lucky for us," Floyd said, wagging his head. "Old Tom'd've skinned us alive if we'd lost them critters. Eh, Pete?"

"*Seguro,*" the *vaquero* agreed solemnly. "He would have been one very mad *hombre.*"

Jess reached for his cigarette makings, tossed the packet to Floyd. "Things like this happen often around here?"

Gonzales watched his partner fill a small paper trough with tobacco grains, then reached for the sack. "*Sí,* it happens too often," he replied, and began to roll a smoke for himself.

Ed Floyd sucked deeply on his cigarette, exhaled a thin cloud. "You looking for work? Reckon Tom could use a man . . . and, seeing the way you handled things just now, you sure ain't no greenhorn."

Holloway shook his head, leaned forward,

and retrieved his makings from the *vaquero.* "Got a job," he said, building his own smoke. "On my way to it now."

"Stranger in these parts?"

"Rode through a couple of times. Recollect hearing about trouble last time I was by . . . Clay Allison and the people who bought up the Maxwell property. . . ."

"Farther west," Floyd explained. "Don't bother us none. Good thing. We got our own war going," he added, and glanced at Gonzales.

The Mexican shrugged.

Floyd turned again to Jess. "If you're just riding through, why not take supper with us? Right sure the boss'd like to do something to show his appreciation."

"Forget it," Holloway said. "Just an accident. No man's going to stand by and see cattle slaughtered like that."

"An honest man wouldn't," Floyd corrected. "Where're you headed?"

"Morrel's place . . . the Slash M. His wife . . . widow sent for me."

Jess was instantly aware of the change in the two riders. Ed Floyd frowned, leaned forward slightly. "You aiming to work for the Slash M?"

"That's what I figure . . . leastwise, I guess I am. I won't know much about it until I talk to Missus Morrel."

Gonzales plucked the half smoked cigarette from his lips, flipped it contemptuously to the ground, spat. A stillness settled over Floyd's face.

"Something about that bother you?" Holloway asked quietly.

Floyd dropped his smoke to the ground. "Obliged to you again," he said coldly, ignoring the question. "Reckon Pete and me'd better get back to work."

Irritation stirred Jess as the chill became more pronounced. "Which way to Morrels'?" he asked, his manner equally distant.

"North. Just keep riding," Ed Floyd answered. "You're on Box K range now, but we'll sort of overlook that. Guess we owe you that much."

"You don't owe me anything," Holloway snapped, "except maybe some explanations."

The cowpuncher shrugged. "Best get your explaining done at the Morrels'."

"Meaning what?"

"Meaning there ain't exactly good feelings between the Lindseys and them."

"Something I didn't know."

"I realize that. Big reason why Pete and me ain't running you off Box K range. You're a stranger around here, and you done us a favor. Calls for some understanding on our part . . . and we're doing just that. Only thing, don't stretch the point. Just move on."

Jess considered the words, nodded curtly. "Fair enough . . . but don't change your mind once I get started. I don't run off easy."

"Figured that, but don't worry none. We don't go changing our word like some people do. Ain't likely you'll be bothered, but if you do run into some of our boys, tell them Ed Floyd said you could cross. They'll leave you be."

"Appreciate that," Jess said, and moved off. "Hope I can return the favor some day."

Floyd gave him a cool, level glance. "Be freezing in hell before I'd let you," he said, and turned away.

III

Jess was not aware of the moment when he crossed onto Morrel range. He knew of that only when he came upon a fair-size herd of cattle all bearing the Slash M brand, grazing in a deep swale where a scatter of cottonwoods clustered around a sink hole.

Saul had chosen well, Holloway thought, as he pulled to a halt at the edge of the water and allowed the roan to slake his thirst. The land was rolling with many natural shelters, and was covered with good grass. There was little snakeweed — always a sign of poor country — and, while no stream was visible in any direction, green trees here and there indicated the presence of underground springs.

He rode on, wondering how many acres Morrel had claimed and if it were all similar to what he was crossing; if so, his old friend had left a fine ranch to his wife. A fine ranch — and apparently a legacy of trouble, he amended. But he guessed that was to be expected; a man worked hard to get what he wanted, and then harder to hold onto it.

He caught his first glimpse of the Slash M proper an hour later when the roan gained a low rise and he looked down into a valley, green with grass and trees. He halted, caught up by the quiet beauty of it.

The main house was long, rambled somewhat as though it had witnessed several additions. Flowers laid bright splashes against its walls and a dense vine of some sort covered most of the north side. Behind it were other buildings — kitchen and dining quarters, the bunkhouse, various sheds, corrals, and finally the barn. Again a feeling of admiration passed through him; Saul had done the job up right.

He loped down the slope and passed under the high crossbeam of the gate into which the Slash M brand had been burned, and drew in at the hitch rack fronting the house. Dismounting, he looped the roan's leathers around the shaved pole and, crossing to the door, knocked sharply. Removing his hat, he stepped back.

Somewhere behind the house a woman was singing, the words in Spanish, the tune a lilting border melody. A hammer was ringing against an anvil in the barn, and farther over in the trees a dog was barking frantically at something he had cornered.

There was a sound at the door. Holloway turned, faced a young man. It was like looking at a twenty-year-old version of Saul — the same sandy hair, light eyes, high cheek bones. He had been right — there was a son.

"I'm Holloway," Jess said. "I expect you're Dave."

"I am," the younger man said in a reserved voice.

Jess waited for him to say more. When it was not forthcoming and Dave made no offer to admit him, Holloway said: "Is your mother home? I got a letter from her."

Dave Morrel nodded, pushed open the

175

screen door. "I'll call her," he said.

Jess stepped into the room — the parlor evidently. It was crowded with heavy furniture — leather-covered chairs, a massive table with carved legs, a large footstool. Framed pictures were on the walls, and above the door leading farther into the house was the mounted head of an elk.

Jess paused in the center of the room, watched Dave disappear into the hallway. He did not mind the resentment in the boy's manner, nor did it surprise him. In Dave's boots he probably would dislike the idea of an outsider being called in to take over the operation of the ranch, too — if that was what Marie Morrel had in mind.

She appeared a moment later, a graying, prim woman of stocky build somewhere in her mid-fifties. She wore a gingham dress and a red-checked apron upon which she was wiping her hands. Halting, she looked Jess up and down frankly.

"So you're Holloway," she murmured.

There was both disapproval and hostility in her tone. Jess felt anger lift within him.

She motioned to one of the chairs. "Sit down, Holloway."

Jess moved to an overstuffed leather rocker, stood beside it until Marie had seated herself. As he sat down, Dave emerged from the hall, standing near the doorway.

"Took you long enough," the woman said. "My husband's been dead three months."

"You sent the letter to Arizona. I'd moved on to Texas," Jess explained. "It had to catch up with me."

Marie Morrel tightened her thin lips. "You might as well know now . . . I wasn't in favor of sending for you. I don't think it's necessary. Dave and I can run the ranch."

Holloway flicked the son with his glance. "A place the size of this can be a lot of work. Too much for a woman . . . and a boy."

"Dave's twenty-one," she snapped. "Not a boy any longer. Saul never seemed to realize that."

Jess opened his mouth and was about to reply that the count of years often meant nothing, that it was ability and the desire to assume responsibility a man must take into consideration, but he let it go unsaid; his welcome was far from cordial without his making it worse.

"It was Saul's wish, just before he died, that I send for you . . . hire you on as foreman until Dave was able to take over."

Holloway nodded. "How did it happen?"

"Gored. He was with the men rounding up strays. His horse stumbled, threw him

177

against a steer. The brute turned on him before he could get out of the way."

That sounded like Saul, right in the middle of the job, doing the hardest and most dangerous part. He was never one to back off, let someone else take the chances.

"Sorry to hear about it. He was a good man . . . and my best friend."

"You should've been his son!" Dave Morrel cut in sarcastically. "The way he was always yammering about you . . . how you could handle cattle, and ride and shoot. I got sick of hearing about you, Holloway!"

Jess said nothing. The chore that lay ahead was not going to be pleasant or easy — that was plain. Dave hated his guts. And Saul's widow resented him. Those were fine conditions under which to work!

"The way I understand it, you want me to be your foreman."

"My husband wanted it. . . ."

"All right, Saul wanted me to take over the place. . . ."

"Up to a point. You'll remember that I own the ranch, that I'm the final word on everything."

"That could make things a bit hard to manage."

"It's up to you. What I want understood is that I own Slash M . . . that my son Dave is owner, too. Someday soon he'll take over, so he's to have something to say about how things are done."

Jess shook his head. "It won't work. You can't have three foremen trying to run one ranch."

"Then don't take the job," Dave suggested quickly.

Holloway shifted his glance to the boy, studied him quietly. "I expect that's what you'd like."

"You can bet on it."

Holloway swore softly to himself. He should get up and walk out right there. He wasn't wanted by Marie Morrel or her son — and he would get damned little co-operation from them in the future; in fact, there would be only opposition. Under such conditions running the Slash M would be virtually an impossibility. But Saul had wanted him to take over — apparently had insisted upon it.

He couldn't let Saul down regardless of the problems. They had been friends too long.

He smiled faintly at Dave, placed his attention on Marie. "I came here hoping I could be of help to you. Wanted to, in fact. It's plain you'd as soon I'd keep riding."

He paused, waiting for Marie Morrel to

comment. She remained silent.

"Well, I can't accommodate you. Saul was my friend. He sent for me and said I was to take over. Maybe it's like getting orders from the grave, but that doesn't matter. I aim to do what he wanted. It's up to you to make the best of it."

Marie shrugged indifferently. Dave said: "You won't like it here, Holloway. I can promise you that."

Jess pulled himself upright. "Try that shoe on the other foot . . . could be you'll be the one who won't like it."

"It's my ranch!" Dave shouted, taking a step forward. "By God, you better remember that!"

"I'll be remembering one thing only," Holloway said, rising. "Your pa sent for me. I figure I'll be working for him, so I'll do things the way I think he'd want them done."

He reached the door, laid his fingers on the latch, paused. Looking back, he said: "I'd like to be friends with both of you, but if you won't have it, then we'll just make the best of what's left."

Marie Morrel rose, folded her hands together beneath her apron. Her eyes were bright with anger.

"As Dave said, you won't like it around

here. My suggestion is to keep going. I'll pay you a month's wages for your trouble. And you'll find a job . . . plenty of them to be had."

A perverse smile tugged at Jess Holloway's lips. "I like this place fine," he said. "Where're my quarters?"

She gave him a brief, furious glance, and started to turn away. "Cabin at the end of the bunkhouse," she said, and moved off into the hall.

Jess returned to the yard. Inwardly he was furious at the reception he had experienced but stubbornness would not permit him to back down — that and a deep loyalty to Saul Morrel. The rancher would not have sent for him — knowing both his wife and son opposed the move — if he had lacked good reason.

He pulled free the roan's leathers and started around the house to his quarters. The woman, possibly the cook, had stopped singing, but the blacksmith still worked in his shed, the clanging of his tools a bright, hard sound in the hot stillness.

He reached the yard behind the house, turned left. An old cowpuncher, lean, gray, and with a trailing handlebar mustache and watery eyes, glanced up from the trough where he had halted with his horse. He stared, grinned, said: "Howdy!"

Jess hesitated. It was the first — and only — show of friendliness he had encountered since arriving at the Slash M. He returned the greeting, started to ask further directions, and then came to sudden attention.

Two men had come from the bunkhouse. They stopped abruptly, hard gaze on him. It was the pair he had driven off at the butte — Nemo and Red.

IV

Red hooked his thumbs in his gun belt as a slow grin spread across his face. Nemo folded his arms across his chest, waited. A strip of white rag encircled the area just below his right elbow where Holloway's bullet had grazed. A third man came from the bunkhouse, a large, thick-shouldered, heavy-featured individual. He paused momentarily, then moved up beside the others.

"What's eating you two?"

Red pointed to Holloway with his chin. "It's the pilgrim . . . the one that stuck his nose in our business. Looks like Dave's hired him on."

The big man raked Jess with a cold glance. "He got a name?"

"Who cares?" Red said softly. "It's going

to pleasure me a lot to teach him a few things."

In the warm hush Holloway eyed the three riders narrowly. The reaction of Ed Floyd and the *vaquero,* Gonzales, made sense now. He faced the old cowpuncher, watching silently from the water trough.

"Do they work for the Slash M?"

"Sort of. Redhead's called Red. Little one's. . . ."

"Met them. Who's the other?"

"Walt Zurcher. Kind of heads up the bunch . . . along with Dave. Special friends of his."

"Stay out of this, old man!" Zurcher warned suddenly, moving forward.

The older cowpuncher stiffened, glanced frowningly at Jess, and then resumed his place at the trough. His weathered face had blanched and hatred burned in his eyes. Jess allowed the roan's reins to drop, squared himself gently to meet Zurcher and the others, pressing in slowly.

"Don't think you're going to like working here, saddlebum," Zurcher drawled, coming to a halt. "If you crawl up on that blue and keep going, reckon we could forget about that long nose of yours."

"That's the second time I've heard that," Holloway replied. "The answer's still no."

He motioned to Nemo and Red. "Are they taking orders from you?"

Zurcher nodded. "Same as everybody else around here."

"I hadn't heard you were the foreman."

The big man laughed. "Maybe I don't wear no sign hanging around my neck, but I sure call the shots . . ."

"You've called your last one," Holloway cut in sharply. "I want you . . . all of you . . . off this ranch in ten minutes. And take anybody else who thinks you're running things."

Walt Zurcher's jaw sagged. Nemo and Red stared. After a long moment Zurcher said — "How's that?" — in a strangled tone.

"You heard it. Get off Slash M range and stay off. If I ever find you on the property again, you've got trouble."

"Mister . . . you've got it right now!" Zurcher shouted angrily, and lunged.

Jess Holloway, expecting the move, was prepared. He stepped lightly to one side. As Zurcher rushed in, he drove a hard, downsledging blow to the man's jaw. Shocked, Walt went to his knees.

From the tail of his eye, Jess saw Red and Nemo surge forward, crouched, ready to take a hand. He half turned to meet them, relaxed as the old cowpuncher's cracked voice cut through the hush.

"Reckon that'll be close enough," he said, waggling a Colt in his horny hand. "This here argument's betwixt Mister Holloway, the new foreman, and Walt."

Jess threw a glance at the older man, wondering how he could have known his name and purpose; he guessed Saul Morrel had mentioned it. Nemo and the redhead fell back a few steps. Jess swung his attention around to Zurcher, now picking himself up.

The big man shook his head, glared at Holloway. "You just bought yourself six feet in the graveyard, cowboy," he snarled, and lunged again.

This time Jess did not pull aside, but instead moved straight into the oncoming man. He threw a stiff left that caught Zurcher flushly on the mouth and stalled him, then crossed with a hard right that cracked like a whip when it landed.

Zurcher rocked, howled. The blow would have dropped an ordinary man, but he recovered, rushed in swinging. Jess took two hard smashes to the belly, a third to the jaw — felt himself stumbling backwards. He steadied himself, jerked to one side, and drove a hard right to Walt's ear.

Zurcher yelled in pain again, lurched to

his left, and stumbled into Holloway. Instantly his thick arms wrapped themselves around Jess's waist. Holloway, caught unawares, struggled to break free as Zurcher began to wrestle him about the yard.

Red yelled something and Holloway felt himself being spun around. Zurcher's death-like grip released and, off balance, he started falling. He half-righted himself, then again felt arms encircle his body and he was thrown against Red.

Walt Zurcher shouted, rushed in, fists swinging. Helpless, Jess took a half dozen rock-hard blows to the belly and ribs — a solid right to the jaw. His senses reeled and he was vaguely conscious of the old cow-puncher yelling something and moving up beside him.

He saw Zurcher coming in again, but his mind was clearing rapidly. He threw his weight against Red, lifted his leg, and caught Walt in the chest with a booted foot. The big man staggered, went to one knee as Red, fighting to regain his balance, tripped and fell, losing his grip on Holloway.

Jess spun, anger roaring through him, and charged Zurcher. As the man came upright, Holloway drove him again to one knee with a hammering flurry of rights and lefts, and finished it off with a hard uppercut. Zurcher sagged, gasped for breath, began to sink. As Walt faded, Jess wheeled to face Red.

He nailed the redhead with a sharp blow to the ear, sent him sprawling into the dust. Ungoverned rage still gripping him, he whirled again, took a long stride toward Nemo. The little gunman fell back, shaking his head.

"I ain't mixing in this. Not my way of doing things."

Heaving for breath, Holloway halted. He pointed at the pistol hanging at the man's hip.

"That your way?"

Nemo stared, shrugged. "Maybe . . . but not now."

"Then drop that iron on the ground and walk off. I don't fancy a bullet in my back."

Nemo obediently drew his weapon, let it fall to the dust, and moved away. The old cowpuncher grinned at Holloway, rubbed nervously at his chin.

"They sort of took me by surprise. . . ."

"Keep your eye on him," Jess said, glancing at Nemo, and then turned back to the others.

Red was sitting up. Zurcher was on hands and knees, head hung low. His mouth was blared open as he sucked hard for breath and a trickle of blood was coming from a corner of his lips.

Holloway stepped to his side, grasped him by the arm, and pulled him to his feet. Walt's eyes had a glazed, unseeing look. Jess turned to the redhead.

"Get up!"

Red drew himself stiffly upright. Holloway, whirling Zurcher around, shoved him at the rider.

"Load him on his horse and move out!"

Red, holding up the heavier man with difficulty, swore angrily. "Dave'll have something to say about this."

"Dave's got nothing to say about it," Holloway snarled. "I'm running this outfit . . . and I don't want you or your kind around."

"Dave. . . ."

"Forget it. And when your partner comes to, remind him of what I said about staying off Slash M range."

Red nodded violently. "I'll tell him . . . and you can be god-damned sure it won't be the end of it."

Jess, the hard core of anger gone, his heaving lungs back to normal, smiled, shrugged. "He knows where to find me."

He turned, touched the two riders who were standing on the bunkhouse porch with a look, crossed to where Nemo's gun lay. Picking it up, he tossed it to the gunman.

"Now the time?"

Nemo hesitated only a moment, and then shook his head. Jamming the weapon into its holster, he crossed to where Red waited, and, taking the dazed Zurcher by his free arm, lent his support to the redhead in getting Walt to his horse.

V

Trusting none of the three men, Jess Holloway stood in the center of the yard, watched them mount up and depart. When they had gone, he turned. The two riders no longer stood on the bunkhouse porch but the old cowpuncher was just behind him.

"By dingies," the man said in his high voice, "Saul said you was the kind to get things done. Sure knowed what he was talking about."

Jess's tall shape relaxed as the last of the harsh tension ebbed from his body, leaving only the dull aches where Walt Zurcher's blows had fallen.

"Sounds like you expected me."

"Sure did. Saul told me all about you . . . how you and him used to do things. Figured it was you when I seen you coming around the house. Watching you brace Zurcher and them two sidewinders proved it."

Holloway moved to where the roan waited patiently, gathered up the leathers. "Have you been around here a long time?"

"Since the beginning. Name's Art Gurney."

Jess thrust out his hand, grasped that of the old cowpuncher. "I remember Saul speaking of you. I guess it was you who got things started for him."

Gurney nodded. "Reckon I'm like one of them sheds . . . sort of a fixture." He sobered. "Expect you know what you're doing . . . running Walt and them others off the place. Dave and his ma ain't going to like it."

"I doubt if they're going to much like anything I do."

Gurney chuckled. "It seems you've already done some palavering with Marie and the boy."

"I have," Jess said, and started toward a small house just beyond the crew's quarters. "If you've got time, I'd like to talk. There're some questions I need answered."

The old cowpuncher bobbed his head happily. "Yes, sir, Mister Holloway."

"Jess. . . ."

"Yes, sir . . . Jess. Be right pleased."

They reached the foreman's cabin. Gurney entered, opening the windows to release the trapped heat while Holloway removed his blanket roll and saddlebags from his horse. Stepping into the room moments later, Jess halted, looked around. His quarters contained only a bed, a table with a cracked lamp, and a chair. The floor and walls were bare.

"I've seen jails that were more comfortable," he observed, tossing his gear onto the bed.

Gurney grinned. "Ain't nobody lived in here for the past two, three years. Saul run things hisself when he was alive. Didn't have no use for a foreman. I'll see iffen the cook can't sort of fix things up a mite."

Holloway leaned against the wall, drew out his cigarette makings. He offered the packet to Gurney but the man declined.

"Get mine chawin'," he said, and dug a plug of dark tobacco from his pocket.

Jess began to roll his smoke. "Where do Zurcher and the two with him fit?" he asked.

"Dave sort of took up with them about a year ago. Saul never had no use for them, told Dave so. The boy didn't pay him no mind. Always was kind of headstrong and done what he pleased. Always figured Saul was too easy on him. And his ma. . . ."

"Has Zurcher got a ranch around here?"

Gurney shifted his cud. "Zurcher? Nope,

he ain't got nothing. Just hangs around the Mulehead Saloon in town when he ain't up to some devilment."

"Same go for Red and Nemo?"

"Same. Three of a kind. Sort of wormed their way in with Dave, got him thinking he's big shakes and they're his best friends. They want him running the place so's they'll have it soft." Gurney hesitated, frowned. "I recollect you saying you'd met Nemo and Red afore. Where at?"

"On my way here . . . early this morning. Stopped them from driving some Box K cattle over a cliff," Jess replied, and related the entire incident.

When he was finished, Art Gurney sighed deeply. "Sure the way they'd do something, all right. Saul and Tom Lindsey had been on the outs for quite a spell, but shenanigans like that never started till Dave began hanging out with Zurcher."

"What caused the trouble?"

Gurney scrubbed at his chin. "Take some remembering. Wasn't much, as I recollect. Some little old piddling thing about the range, I think. But you know how a grudge sort of grows, gets worse. Families was once mighty close."

"And Zurcher's doing his best to keep the fire going."

"Sure is . . . and Dave's right in there with him."

Holloway frowned, flipped his spent cigarette through the open doorway. "Can't figure Dave. I thought maybe he was just young, trying to show how big he is. Wouldn't think he'd side with Zurcher or anybody else in killing cattle and things like that."

"He'll go along with whatever Walt tells him he ought to do. Zurcher's got him wrapped around his thumb. My hunch is old Walt figures he can someday own this here spread if he plays his cards . . . meaning Dave . . . right."

Saul must have seen that, too, Jess thought. That would account for the rancher's insisting that Marie hire him on as foreman.

"You know if this is the first time Zurcher tried to stampede Box K cattle over the butte?"

"Hard telling. Been a lot of cussedness and pure meanness on both sides. Shooting calves, poisoning water holes, burning line shacks . . . lot of other things including just plain rustling. It's getting so a man can't even get his chores done."

Holloway crossed to the bed, began to unwrap his belongings. "Looks like first thing I better do is start patching things up with this Tom Lindsey. Sure can't run a ranch with a war going on."

"Be natural," Gurney said, "only you ain't going to find it that easy. Tom's a mighty contrary critter when he wants to be."

"I've got an edge . . . saving that stock for him. He ought to be willing to hear me out."

"Sure ought. You want me trailing along?"

"I'd better handle it alone. I got the idea Slash M riders aren't welcome on Box K land."

"That's for sure, but you. . . ."

"Nobody knows me yet except the one they call Ed Floyd and a *vaquero,* Pete Gonzales."

"Ed's Tom Lindsey's foreman . . . right nice feller. Me and him used to pal around some. Don't know the Mex . . . probably new. Zurcher makes it hard for Tom to keep help."

Holloway paused, looking squarely at Art Gurney. "I'm still not sure about some things. Why do you figure Saul insisted on his wife sending for me? Are there other problems besides Lindsey and Dave?"

The old cowpuncher cocked his head to one side. "Weren't because of Tom Lindsey. Saul was the kind who could live another fifty years without even speaking to him if he'd been of a mind. And it was just little things that started between them. I figure it's Dave . . . only thing that makes sense. I think it was because he'd just got this here place built up to where it was a real fine outfit, ready to make big money, and then that danged steer got him.

"He was afraid the whole thing would go down a hole if there wasn't somebody around with sense and guts enough to carry things on the way they ought. He was smart enough to see Dave couldn't do it . . . and he had Walt Zurcher figured out, too. Probably guessed Walt would cheat the boy out of the whole spread before too long.

"So he sent for you. He told me a dozen times how the pair of you done your thinking alike, always somehow had the same ideas. Saul had a powerful lot of faith in you, Jess, and last thing he said to me afore he died was that I was to stand by you when you showed up."

"I'm obliged to you for that," Holloway murmured. "Counting up, I've got exactly one friend in the Cimarron country . . . you."

"Be more'n just me, come dark. Them two 'punchers standing on the porch seen you mop up the ground with Walt and Red, and then back Nemo off. Whole crew'll know about it by supper. We've all been hoping a day like this'n would come along. Marie hard-mouth you considerable?"

"Made it plain I wasn't wanted . . . or needed."

"Well, you'll sort of have to overlook a lot of what she says. She thinks there ain't nothing like her boy, Dave. Expect that's how it is with most women."

"You believe Saul would want me to go ahead and do what I figure's right whether she's for it or not?"

"Know danged well he would!"

"She still owns the place. . . ."

"Makes no difference. Kinda like a horse fighting medicine . . . sometimes you got to force them for their own good."

Jess Holloway sighed, tossed his empty saddlebags into a corner. "That's the way I look at it, too. I just wanted to be sure." He stared at the smoked chimney of the lamp with its half-moon crack. "I can think of a lot of things I'd rather do than buck a proud mama and her pride and joy."

"Reckon that's what it amounts to," Gurney said, moving to look through the window. "Here comes Dave . . . and he's sure foaming at the mouth."

VI

Jess settled back against the table. Arms crossed, he waited. Moments later Dave Morrel appeared in the doorway. His face was flushed and his eyes snapped angrily. He gave Art Gurney a hard, passing glare, came into the room, and halted in front of Holloway.

"What the hell's this I hear about you firing Walt Zurcher and a couple more of my hired hands?"

"They're fired. Nothing else to it," Jess replied coolly.

"You're hiring them back. . . ."

Holloway shook his head. "No. And if I find any more of their kind around, I'll get rid of them, too."

Dave's face whitened. "Their kind? What's that mean?"

"Saloon bums . . . tramps. None of them ever turned a day's work in his life."

"Been doing all right up to now."

"At what? Running Box K cattle over buttes?"

Morrel stared. "What was that?"

"You heard me . . . and there'll be no men like that working on the Slash M as long as I'm running it." Jess paused, looked more closely at Dave. "You trying to say you didn't know about it?"

Morrel shrugged. "I've been looking after this place. I know what my men do."

"Figured you did," Holloway said. "Could be you were one of the two who suckered the Box K boys off while Red and Nemo got the stock to running. You and Zurcher, maybe. . . ."

"Anything they done was for the good of the ranch. . . ."

"You know better than that," Jess said in disgust. "That kind of neighbor sniping never settled anything . . . just made things worse and kept a feud going. I aim to put a stop to it."

"You keep out of it! It's not your business. . . ."

"It sure as hell is my business when it affects the ranch! No place makes any money when it's all riled up and hunting trouble."

"Lindsey's as much at fault as we are!" Dave flared.

"Could be, but that's not the point. It's hurting Slash M . . . same as it is the Box K. Your pa realized that, and was probably going to do something about it when that steer gored him. He was too smart to stomp his own toes. And it's going to get worse unless we get rid of the Walt Zurchers and

198

come to an understanding with Tom Lindsey."

"How do you figure to do that? Lindsey
won't talk to you."

"I sure aim to try."

Dave wheeled impatiently, moved to the
door. "You'll be wasting your time. Anyway,
who says you're right? Who says we want
things patched up with him?"

"I say it," Holloway replied bluntly.

"We don't need Lindsey . . . just in the
way. The sooner he realizes that and sells
out, the better things will be."

Jess studied Morrel thoughtfully. "So
that's the way it is. Whose idea . . . yours or
Zurcher's?"

Dave flushed angrily. "Mine!"

"Maybe," Holloway said softly. "Makes no
difference . . . forget it."

"I'm still owner of this ranch . . . running
it."

"Not any more. Better get that straight,
Dave."

"You can't come horsing in here. . . ."

"It wasn't my idea. If you were half the
man your pa had been hoping for, I'd not
be here now."

Dave Morrel's eyes snapped as anger
surged through him. His lips parted as
though he were about to make a scathing

reply, and then clamped shut. Abruptly he wheeled and moved through the doorway.

Gurney pulled his lank shape erect, crossed to the window. He watched Morrel until he had reached the corner of the main house and was lost to view. He turned then to Jess.

"You sure twisted the knife in him that time."

Holloway shrugged. "I don't like doing it, but it's about time somebody made him face up. How far is it to Lindsey's?"

"Close to three hours' riding. You going there now?"

"Why not? Sooner I talk to him, sooner things will start easing off."

Gurney wagged his head. "Got to side with Dave on that. Misdoubt if Tom'll even listen to you."

"I've got to start somewhere," Jess said wearily.

"Ain't so sure it's safe. Box K 'punchers won't be the only ones wanting to take a pot shot at you . . . there's Zurcher and his crowd. He won't be giving up."

"His kind never does," Holloway grunted, moving toward the door. "Which way?"

"Head southwest. Just keep going, you'll run smack into Lindsey's."

Jess nodded, crossed to where the roan

was tied. He gave the blue a quick appraisal, decided there was no need to change horses; the roan had not traveled far and was still in good condition.

He swung to the saddle, touched the brim of his hat in salute to Gurney, and wheeled about. Marie Morrel appeared suddenly at the corner of the house, was moving toward him. Jess sighed, drew to a halt.

"Here's where I get the other barrel," he said to Gurney, and came down from the saddle.

The widow stopped before him, fixed him with her angry gaze. "I've been talking to Dave," she said, allowing that to explain everything.

Holloway removed his hat, waited for her to continue. She was the one with the problem.

"He tells me you fired Walt Zurcher, along with Red and Nemo . . . all of them his friends. When he asked you to let them come back, he says you refused."

"They stay fired," Holloway said. "Can't trust men like that. They stop at nothing, and one day they'll cut your throat."

"Did you fire them because they were friends of Dave?"

"That had nothing to do with it. I got rid of them because I don't want them around."

Marie dropped her eyes. "He tells me you're going to talk to Tom Lindsey."

"I was on my way when you came up."

"I can't see that it will do any good."

"Dave's thinking, too. Guess I'll have to find out for myself."

"What if I tell you I don't want you to go crawling over there . . . begging him?"

"I'm not crawling, and I sure don't aim to beg. This is as important to him as it is to us. Just want to iron things out."

"I can order you not to go!"

"I'll do it, anyway, Missus Morrel. I've got to do what I think is right."

"And you won't let Dave bring Walt and the others back?"

"I've already answered that. I'm giving word to all the hands that they're to run them off if they ever find them on Slash M range. Shoot, if need be."

Marie Morrel stiffened. "That's a bit high-handed."

"Maybe it is," Jess replied, a trace of impatience in his tone. Suddenly he was weary of it all — of the bickering, the arguing, and stubborn opposition. Hooking one arm on his saddle horn, he leaned forward. "Lady, you can fire me right now if you've a mind to. I can't stop it. But your husband wanted me to take on this job and do it the best I know how. I'm trying to do just that. What I want to know now is are you going to keep bucking me, or are you going to let me do things my way?"

Marie glanced at Art Gurney, brought her attention back to Holloway. "Saul wanted you here," she murmured.

"And for a danged good reason!" Gurney declared. "Give him his head. Let him do what he figures is needful."

"I don't need your advice!" she snapped.

"Well, you're getting it anyway," the old cowpuncher said, tempering the harsh words with a grin. "Saul done a lot of talking to me about Holloway. It won't be no mistake, letting him run things for a spell."

Marie's expression did not change. Her lips were a thin, set line as she faced Jess.

"You're doing this without my consent. I want you to understand that, Holloway. But go ahead, if it's what you want."

"And Zurcher?"

"Hiring and firing is a foreman's job."

Jess smiled. He had made some progress, won at least one victory, however small. "Obliged to you, ma'am," he said. "If that's all, I expect I'd better be on my way."

Marie Morrel nodded, turned, and started for the house. Jess glanced at Art Gurney. The old cowpuncher grinned broadly, lifted his hand.

"So long, boy. Keep your eyes peeled!"

"I'll do that," Holloway replied, and headed the roan out of the yard.

VII

He reached Tom Lindsey's Box K Ranch late in the afternoon. As he pulled to a halt at the edge of the hard-packed yard, he allowed his eyes to probe the cluster of well-kept buildings, halting finally on the main house.

An elderly man, a woman of like age, and a girl were sitting on the porch. It was near the supper hour and they apparently awaited the cook's summons to the meal. Elsewhere, he could see riders lounging in the shade, apparently also awaiting the clang of the triangle.

Jess gave them a swift survey, hopeful of spotting either Ed Floyd or the *vaquero,* Pete Gonzales. Neither man was present. He would be strictly on his own, without any favorable recommendation. He had kept his eyes open for the foreman and the Mexican rider all the way from Morrels', planning to ask them for an introduction to the rancher, but he had seen only three horsemen during the long journey, and they at considerable distance.

Squaring himself on the saddle, he moved out of the windbreak bordering the yard and walked the roan slowly toward the house. Two or three of the nearby cowpunchers immediately came to life. Tom Lindsey glanced up, his broad, florid face pulled into a frown.

Holloway stopped the blue at the rail, removed his hat, and said: " 'Evening."

The rancher continued to stare. The girl looked up with interest while the older woman, Lindsey's wife apparently, worked at something she was knitting.

" 'Evening," Lindsey replied finally in a gruff voice.

Jess could feel the man's eyes digging into him, taking note of his equipment, of the brand the blue wore on his shoulder. He remained motionless, waiting for an invitation to dismount. It did not come.

"Name's Holloway," he said. "I work for the Morrels."

"I know that," Lindsey cut in roughly. "What do you want?"

"Talk."

The rancher shook his head. "What about? We got nothing to draw on."

"I figure there's plenty," Jess said, his own voice hard-edged. "Mind if I step down?

It's been a long ride."

"Up to you," Lindsey said indifferently.

Holloway swung from the roan, anchored him to the hitch rack, and moved forward to the edge of the porch. From the corner of his eye he saw several Box K riders closing in silently from both sides, their expressions intent, suspicious.

One foot on the step, hat in hand, he faced Tom Lindsey. The rancher was about the same age as Saul Morrel would be he guessed — and much like him: stubborn, proud, and probably honest. Mrs. Lindsey appeared younger than Marie Morrel, however, and still showed traces of girlhood beauty. The daughter would be Dave's age — dark, blue-eyed, well-shaped.

"Said you knew me . . . ," he began.

"Ed Floyd told me about the cattle. Obliged to you . . . but the favor don't call for no special treatment. Expect you didn't know what you were doing . . . and as far as I'm concerned, you're just another of the Morrel crowd."

"Not exactly," Holloway said coolly. "I'm working for the Slash M, and I'm not one of the crowd, as you name it. Saul had his wife send for me to take over when he saw he wasn't going to make it. That's what I'm doing."

Mrs. Lindsey ceased her knitting, dropped her hands in her lap, and looked up. She was frowning.

"It still means you're working for Marie Morrel and that son of hers," the rancher insisted.

"Working for myself, or for Saul, you could say. And first thing I've got in mind to do is straighten out this trouble between you folks and the Slash M."

"Be a mite hard to undo."

"Maybe. Don't know what it's all about, and I don't much care. From what I've heard, it's a lot of little things that got snowballed into something big."

"Little things!" Lindsey shouted, hoarse and angry. "Driving off stock, burning trail grass, shooting calves . . . you call them little things?"

Holloway shook his head. "I sure don't. But I expect the Morrels could do some fussing, too. The point is, I'm here to end it . . . to get everybody to forget what's happened so's we can both get down to ranching in peace."

Lindsey tugged at his mustache. "It can't be done. There's been too much that's happened, and I ain't the forgetting kind."

"I'm not asking you to forget, just to let things ride and not kick up any more trouble. I'll do the same. Slash M riders will stay in line if your Box K men will."

"Hogwash!" Lindsey said in a voice filled with disgust. "How you going to control a bunch of hardcases like's hanging around your place?"

"I can," Holloway said quietly. "There'll be no more stampedes, or anything else like that as long as I'm running the ranch. You've got my word. I'd like the same guarantee from you."

"Ain't promising nothing," Lindsey said flatly. "Be a waste of breath." He looked at Jess sharply. "The Morrels know you're here?"

Holloway nodded.

"They send you?"

"It was my idea."

"But they wasn't for it, I'm betting. Not them two."

"It makes no difference whether they were or not."

"The hell it don't! They own the outfit, don't they? Anything you say, they can back off from, and that's what they'll do. I know the Morrels. They're not. . . ."

"Saul Morrel was the best men I ever met, or knew," Holloway broke in curtly. "I won't stand for any man talking against him. His being dead don't change that."

Lindsey's gaze fell. After a moment, he said: "I was sorry to hear about Saul dying. Real sorry. We used to be good friends, but that woman of his . . . and the boy."

"Your trouble start with Saul or them?"

Lindsey shifted on his chair. "Saul. Couple years ago, more or less."

"The whole thing died with Saul, then. Not much sense carrying it on."

"Nothing's changed. Dave's just like his pa . . . bull-headed."

"It seems to be plentiful on both sides," Holloway said. "The fact is, the Morrels will meet you halfway if you'll give them a chance."

"Did Marie say that?"

"No, not in plain words, but she'll come around once you make a move. Dave, too."

"Mite hard to believe that," the rancher murmured. "And I've been fooled before. Ain't about to lay myself open again."

The iron triangle *clanged,* sent its ringing call echoing through the closing darkness. No one moved.

"What you want me to do?" Lindsey asked, his manner impatient.

"Nothing special," Jess replied, feeling a stir of hope. "Call a truce, a halt on whatever you and your riders have been doing. I'll do the same with the Slash M crew. We'll all settle down and get some ranching done."

Lindsey considered for a moment, then pulled himself stiffly to his feet. "I expect I'd better study on that. Supposing you drop back in a week or two . . . after the drive's over?"

"It was me who made the first move," Jess said, his hopes dying quickly and a quiet stubbornness taking over. "It's only right that you come to the Morrel place if you want to talk more about it."

Lindsey stared at him in amazement. "Ride across Slash M range, get my head shot off? Do you think I'm a damned fool?"

"I took a chance crossing Box K land," Holloway said. "If I can trust your word, you can trust mine."

"Well, I ain't ready to do that yet," Lindsey said, and wheeled abruptly for the door.

Jess watched the rancher jerk open the screened panel and stamp into the room. Mrs. Lindsey rose slowly, smiled apologetically.

"My husband forgot his manners, Mister Holloway. You'll take supper with us?"

Jess shook his head. "Thank you, but I reckon I'd better be getting back to the ranch. It's a long ride."

The woman took an impulsive step closer to the edge of the porch. "Don't judge Tom too hard. He and Saul were like brothers until the trouble came between them. I think he's more hurt than anything."

Holloway nodded. "Yes'm, that and maybe a lot of pride. I'd like for him to see things my way. It would be foolish to let matters run out, get out of hand."

The rancher's wife straightened slightly. "Tom could be right, you know."

"There's right on both sides," Jess said heavily, and, ducking his head politely, turned to the roan.

He swung to the saddle, noting the cowpunchers, still quiet and withdrawn, yet scattered about the yard. He favored them with an impersonal glance, moved off into the night.

VIII

Burning trail grass. . . . That accusation of Tom Lindsey's somehow lodged in Jess Holloway's mind and would not leave. He pondered its meaning — wished he had pressed the rancher for an explanation.

He wondered, too, if he had accomplished anything of value. Lindsey was bitter — that was evident — but, as he had pointed out, likely the Morrels had reason for bitterness, too. It wouldn't be all one-sided; such

211

misunderstandings never were.

But he did feel better. The first move toward peace had been made, and Tom Lindsey was a fair man, if gruff. He'd see the futility of carrying on the feud and act accordingly. Just how Marie Morrel would react when he showed up at the Slash M was something else. He grinned wryly, shrugged. He'd cross that creek when he got to it.

His thoughts came to a sudden halt. Somewhere off to his right he had caught the sound of a horse moving, the muted *thud* of hoofs, the dry scrape of leather against brush. His hand dropped to the pistol at his hip and he glanced hurriedly around. He was in an area of low, brushy hills and shallow arroyos — almost breaks. Buttes loomed up darkly a short distance ahead.

He touched the blue with his spurs, quickened the pace. It was a bad place in which to meet trouble, if that was what lay before him. Abruptly he halted. A rider swung onto the trail, stopped. Again his fingers touched the weapon at his side — and then fell away. It was the girl from the porch at Lindsey's!

"Mister Holloway?" she called quickly.

"Name's Jess," he replied, relief turning his voice sharp. "Could've got yourself shot, sneaking in on me that way."

"I wasn't sneaking!" she answered indignantly as he kneed the roan up to her. "Just happened to cut across the badlands, trying to head you off. I wasn't sure where you'd be. I'm Myra Lindsey."

"The daughter?"

She moved her head. "The daughter. You make it sound like something bad. . . ."

Holloway stirred. "No . . . I didn't mean to, anyway. It's just that this thing between your folks and the Morrels has got me stumped. I'm not sure I got anywhere with your pa." He paused, looked at the girl closely. In the growing moonlight her face was a pale, silver-tinted oval. "Did you follow me for a reason?"

"I want to talk," she said frankly.

"About what? The trouble?"

She nodded, then shook her head. "About Dave, really." Understanding came to Jess Holloway. "Is there something between you and him?"

"There was until all this started. We'd planned to be married by now."

"But your folks wouldn't hear of it."

"Neither would Dave's. And he's changed . . . he's not like he used to be."

"Changed . . . how?"

"Well, he used to be different . . . interested in cattle raising, in the ranch. We made a lot of plans, and everything was fine. Of course, he and his pa never got on good but that was only because Mister Morrel was always insisting Dave do everything just right. I figured it would work out, only it didn't."

"You broke up?"

She nodded. "Dave started hanging around town, the saloon . . . seeing those girls . . . women. . . ."

"It probably happened about the time he took up with Walt Zurcher and his crowd."

"That's it! Zurcher seems to have a lot of influence with him. More than I have, anyway."

"Or anybody else, including his ma and pa. But I think that'll end now. Leastwise, I'm hoping so."

She glanced up at him curiously. "Why?"

"I fired Zurcher today, along with Nemo and Red . . . that pair that's always with him. They won't be hanging around the ranch any more."

Myra's spirits brightened at once. "That's fine! But they were Dave's friends. Didn't he object?"

"Plenty! It didn't do him any good."

"And his mother let you do it?" There was still surprise and a thread of doubt in the girl's tone.

"She didn't like it much, either. We had a few words but it ended up my way."

Myra was quiet for a long minute. Then: "Why didn't you tell my father that?"

Holloway stirred. "I doubt if anything I did or didn't tell him will change him much until he's ready."

"It might have made a difference. He's always figured Walt Zurcher was a bad influence on Dave, blamed him for a lot of the things that happened."

"He's probably right. Zurcher wants to keep things stirred up, but he won't be around now to work at it."

"But Dave can see him in town if he wants to."

Jess shook his head. "That's something I can't stop. I didn't hire out as a nursemaid, and Dave's a grown man. He'll come to his senses one of these days."

Myra brushed a lock of hair from her face. "I hope it won't be too late," she said in a spiritless voice. "Thank you for telling me all this. I . . . I feel better."

He grinned at her. "You sound like it. But don't fret too much. Dave'll be all right, and, if I can help things along, I'll do it."

She gave him a quick smile, and murmuring — "So long." — pulled off into the brush.

Holloway listened to the beat of her horse, until the sound had faded, and then moved on. He glanced ahead to the bluffs. About halfway home, he realized, remembering the trail from the afternoon. Still a long ride before him — and a hungry one. He hoped Art Gurney would remind the cook to hold back some grub. . . .

The trail began to lift toward the foot of the buttes. The brush thinned and the narrow path now wound through piles of boulders, whipped back and forth between scrubby trees. Aware of the climb, Jess let the roan slow his pace.

His thoughts again shifted to Tom Lindsey. He wondered if he had approached the rancher in the wrong way. It might have been better to make deeper inquiries, find out just what had caused the rift between the rancher and Saul Morrel, and then work toward that specific problem. It still might be a good idea. He'd ask Art Gurney about it in the morning, see if he couldn't recall. . . .

Jess Holloway brought the gelding to a halt, a sharp warning suddenly turning him wary. He wasn't sure what it had been, knew only that something was not right. And then it came to him. Ambush!

IX

Holloway heard the quiet *swish* of a rope cutting through the warm hush. His hand swept down for the gun at his hip, halted short when the noose settled around his waist, clamped his arms tight against his body. He spurred forward, trying to get clear, felt a second loop encircle his shoulders. Abruptly he was jerked from the saddle, fell heavily to the ground.

Stunned, he lay there, struggling to collect his senses. He could neither see nor hear anyone, had no idea who the ambushers might be; it could be Walt Zurcher and his crowd — but there was the possibility that some of Lindsey's Box K riders were involved.

That thought sent a gust of anger rushing through him. If true, Myra Lindsey was part of it. She had purposely intercepted and delayed him, enabled the others to set up their trap. He swore, tried to sit up. The ropes jerked savagely, pulling from opposite directions, cutting deeply into his flesh. Gasping with pain, he lay back.

Suddenly he was snapped forward as the

riders at the ends of the ropes began to move toward the buttes. Holloway slewed around sharply, banged his head against a rock. His senses flickered again. Cursing, fighting the two lines, he bounced and scraped against brush and the rocky surface of the trail as he was dragged rapidly along the ground.

Pain slashed at him as a sharp-edged stone gouged into his shoulder; another wave sickened him when an exposed root dug into his side. Furious at his own helplessness, he tried to reach his weapon but his arms were locked tightly to his body and his fingers could barely touch the butt of the pistol.

He tried to see who the riders were, failed. They were too far ahead and the darkness and thick brush made it impossible. Behind him he could make out the roan, however, dimly visible in the dust as he followed.

The surface became rougher. Holloway jolted from side to side as he came up against stiff brush and heavier growth. His head struck something; his mind snapped forward in a shower of lights. He felt himself plunge into a ravine, knew searing pain as he was dragged up the opposite bank. Again his head smashed into an unyielding object. His brain wavered.

He fought to retain consciousness, instinctively continued to struggle against the ropes. A dark wall loomed over him. They had reached the buttes and were now moving along the foot of the formation. Pain eased slightly as the surface of the trail became smoother, cushioned with a thick layer of loose dust.

Out of the brush finally, he caught glimpses of the star-shot sky, an occasional overhanging cedar. His back and shoulders seemed to be on fire and his head was filled with pain from the countless blows it had taken. But he clung grimly to consciousness. His chance to get free of the taut, imprisoning ropes would come. When it did — he must be ready.

Suddenly the night exploded in a flare of light. A terrible rush of pain washed over him as his head came up hard against the cold edge of a rock. He was aware of being thrown to one side with great force, of flopping back, like a fish out of water, and then merciful blackness closed in.

He opened his eyes to intense pain and a peculiar sensation of floating. The ropes still bound him, and his arms, pinned to his sides, were numb. As his fogged brain cleared, he looked about. He was suspended in space. Above him was the star-filled sky, below a rock-studded arroyo. The free ends of the ropes had been anchored at the opposing rims of the deep wash; he had then been thrown over the edge to hang motionlessly.

He struggled briefly, gave it up when spasms of fresh pain gripped him, leaving him breathless. His head sagged forward, relieving some of the strain on his neck muscles. He twisted gently, trying to ease the pressure of the ropes, but his weight was his own enemy and he could find no relief.

He listened then for sounds of the men who had trapped him and could hear nothing but the far-off *hooting* of an owl. Likely they had gone, confident that by daylight he would be dead.

Ignoring the agony, he began to thrash desperately, hopeful of jerking loose one of the ropes from its mooring, disregarding the possibility of death or at least serious injury on the rocks below. Even that would be better than slow strangulation.

Nothing gave. His violent activities served only to draw the ropes tighter and cut more deeply into his body.

His outstretched fingers touched the butt of his pistol, jammed tightly in the holster by dirt and bits of twigs, leaves, and other trash scooped into it while he was being dragged up the slope.

Hope came to him. If he could manage to draw the weapon, turn it sideways enough to shoot one of the ropes in two, he would be making a start toward freedom. He would also permit himself to slam into the side of the butte when the remaining rope, unhindered, swung downward.

But it would be better than just hanging there while life was being choked from his body. Maybe — if he was lucky — he could manage to spin about, take the impact feet first and cushion the shock.

He began to work at drawing the pistol. By swinging back and forth, throwing his legs to the side, he finally managed to wrap his fingers around the butt of the weapon, pull it clear. Then with slow, persistent care, fearful of the pistol slipping from his precarious grasp, he placed it in the palm of his hand.

As his grip tightened about the familiar, worn curves of the cedar handles, he heaved a sigh. That much was done.

Cocking the hammer with his thumb, he twisted the heavy weapon about, pointing it at the rope on his left. The position of the gun in his hand was not firm at such an angle, and he realized he stood a good chance of losing his grip when the concussion came — but he had no choice except to try.

Again checking his aim, he pressed off the shot. The gun bucked wildly in his hand. Powder burned his arm and the flash was blinding, but the rope gave. He turned to it, endeavored to see, but his eyes were blanked by yellow light.

He felt the rope give again. His vision cleared. Several strands of the cord had parted. The bullet had sliced through half the rope, set the frayed ends on fire. Now, a little at a time, the remainder of the rope, unable to support his weight, was parting.

Jess glanced to the slope. It would be a thirty-foot downward swing at least — and momentum would bring him in hard. Unless he could manage to take it feet first he stood the risk of. . . .

He set himself for the impact. It was too late to worry about it now. Another strand of hemp broke. Another — and abruptly he was soaring through the night. Frantically he jerked himself about, tried to check the spinning. He succeeded only partly, crashed into the slope of the arroyo with sickening force, his left leg bearing the brunt of the collision. Breathing heavily, he lay quietly, waiting for the pain to subside.

With the pull of the opposing rope gone, there was a slackness around his waist. Bracing himself with his feet, he lifted upwards, further decreasing the tension. Working his arms, he loosened the noose, pushed it by his shoulders, and found himself free.

His body tingled as circulation renewed. He stood there for several minutes, enduring the discomfort, and then, employing the rope, he drew himself to the rim of the butte. On the crest, and again breathless, he paused to rest and looked around for the roan.

The horse would be nearby, he knew, unless the men who had dropped him over the edge had intentionally led him off. Getting to his feet, he moved down to the trail. The blue was waiting patiently in a pocket of rabbitbrush.

Holloway sighed, climbed onto the saddle. His body was a solid mass of aches, and across his back and shoulders the scratches and cuts, accumulated while he was being dragged, burned with sullen fury.

But he was alive and the fire that scourged his skin from without was no fiercer than the anger that flowed within. Someone would pay for that night's work. Either Zurcher or Tom Lindsey. . . .

X

It was midnight when Jess Holloway finally reached the darkened buildings of Morrel's Slash M and rode onto the hard pack. Numb, so weary he could scarcely stay in the saddle, he crossed to his quarters and halted.

Immediately the door flung open and Art Gurney's lank figure was silhouetted in the rectangle of yellow light.

"Where you been?" the old cowpuncher demanded testily. "You was gone so long I got to worrying. Was about to start out hunting. . . ."

Words died on Gurney's lips. He came to a full stop beside Jess, lower jaw sagging. "Gawdamighty, son," he breathed in an awed tone. "What in the name of tunket happened to you?"

"Ambushed," Holloway muttered thickly and swung stiffly from the roan.

Gurney moved up hurriedly, threw his arm about Jess's shoulders to support him. Holloway winced, swore vividly. The old cowpuncher drew back, staring at his shredded shirt.

"Wonder you ain't dead. In fact, ain't hardly decent, you still being alive."

Jess grinned in spite of himself, started

224

slowly and painfully for the door. Gurney stepped up next to him and, careful where he placed his hands, assisted him into the cabin and onto the bed.

"Now you lay there, quiet like," the older man said. "Got some salve over'n my bunk that'll be just the dope for them cuts and gouges. Got something else you need, too . . . about a half a bottle of rye."

Holloway muttered his appreciation, groaned as he shifted his weight on the hard, corn-husk mattress. Closing his eyes, he dozed, came awake almost immediately as Gurney's heels rapped hollowly against the doorsill. He became aware of the man bending over him, of the cool touch of a bottle being pressed into his hand.

"Pour a speck of that down your throat," Gurney said. "Sort of fix you up whilst I heat some water. Got a right smart of cleaning to do on your back afore I dare rub on the medicine."

The stove in the corner of the room rattled as Gurney set to work building a fire. Jess tipped the neck of the bottle to his lips, took a long drink. The rye was raw, hit bottom like a thunderbolt, leaving him breathless. He groaned, rode out a full minute, and then took a second swallow. A warm glow began to spread through him.

He felt Gurney's fingers upon his back, pulling away the shredded cloth. "Where'd this happen?"

"Close to the buttes," Holloway replied in a low voice. "Caught me in the rocks."

"Sure did work you over some. What's these here red marks . . . sort of like stripes around your middle?"

Jess clamped his teeth to prevent moaning. "Rope burns. Dragged me to the top, then threw me over. Woke up dangling over an arroyo. Managed to shoot one of the ropes in two, to get back here."

Gurney swore softly, crossed to the stove, and returned. A moment later Holloway felt him brushing gently at the cuts with a wet cloth.

"Know who done it?"

Jess shook his head, took another jolt of the rye. His back and shoulders began to sting and he realized Gurney was now applying the salve.

"Zurcher. Or maybe some of the Box K bunch. Never did get a look at them."

The old cowpuncher paused. "What makes you think it could be Lindsey's doings?"

"Only a guess," Holloway replied, and related the interview with the rancher and the encounter with Myra. "She could have set me up for the ambush," he concluded.

Gurney resumed his ministrations. "Could be . . . but Myra's a mighty fine little gal, howsomever. I misdoubt she had anything to do with it, leastwise not that she knowed of. Could've just used her." He hesitated again. "Fact is, it don't sound like Tom a-tall. Was I guessing, I'd say it'd be Zurcher and his crowd."

It was natural for the old cowpuncher to think first of Walt Zurcher and his friends, and place the blame on them. His intense hatred had been apparent earlier.

"Don't see Lindsey stooping to killing," Gurney continued. "And his boys wouldn't take it on themselves. He'd have to order them. Nope, I'll lay you odds it was Zurcher, along with Nemo and Red. You got an old shirt I can tear up for bandages? A couple of places the cuts are pretty deep."

Jess pointed to the clothing piled on the table. "Something in there."

Between the whiskey and Art Gurney's doctoring, he was beginning to feel better. Moving carefully, he rolled over, sat up. His head swam briefly and he remained quiet, allowed the room to stop whirling. When all was once more normal, he faced the old cowpuncher.

"What started this ruckus between Saul

and Lindsey? You said before you couldn't remember. Do some more thinking."

"Did just that," Gurney said, methodically ripping one of Holloway's undershirts into strips. "It was a trail drive that set things off."

"A trail drive?"

"Yep, that was it. See, it's this way. Folks around here take their beef to the railhead at Springer, about five days going. It happens the Morrels and Lindseys follow the same trail.

"Things went along with no trouble first time, but we learned something. The first herd across had the best pickings . . . plenty of grass. Next man sort of got the leavings. Best grazing was gone . . . and what grass was left was all tromped and mighty poor."

"So it got to be a scramble to see who moved his stock first," Holloway said, nodding.

"Just what happened," Gurney said, crossing over and beginning to wind a bandage around Jess's shoulder. "But that weren't the end of it. Some of the hands got to playing cussed tricks, making the thing even worse. Don't think Saul and Tom Lindsey knew about that in the beginning . . . and when they finally did, it was too late to do anything. So things blew up betwixt them, both of them hollering at the other."

Gurney paused, picked up another bandage. "Whole dang' mess fit just right for Walt Zurcher when he blew in. He got himself friendly with Dave who argued his pa into hiring on Walt and Red and Nemo. That bunch sure did make it rough for Lindsey. Reckon last year was the worst of all. . . . You hungry?"

"Sure am," Holloway said impatiently. "Finish what you were saying."

"Well," the older man said, returning once more to the table, "Saul and his crew got off first ahead of Tom. He didn't know about it, but soon's he'd drove his herd through the valley, Dave and Zurcher and them two skunks of his'n rode back and set fire to the grass. When Lindsey come along a couple days later, there weren't nothing but ashes everywhere."

That was what Tom Lindsey had meant when he referred to the trail grass being burned. Jess shook his head. Lindsey had a right to be riled.

"Did Saul say anything to Dave and Zurcher about it?" he asked, wondering if his old friend had changed any in his usual reaction to such a senseless trick.

"He was fit to be tied," Gurney said, handing Jess a plate on which were two pieces of thick steak and several buttered biscuits. "Snuck this from the cook. Cold, but it'll fill your belly."

Holloway grinned his thanks and began to eat hungrily. After a moment he said: "Saul must've changed a lot. If a man had done that a few years ago, he'd have skinned him alive."

"Maybe, but things ain't the same. Dave sort of made out like it was all sort of a prank, that Walt and him didn't mean for it to get out of hand. His ma took up for him against Saul. I reckon that's what really tore the blanket, Marie stepping into the argument. Saul sure thought a heap of that woman. She could do 'most anything she wanted with him."

Holloway was only half listening. His eyes were on the floor as he munched the dry meat and bread. "That valley," he said, not looking up, "is there plenty of grass there for both herds?"

"Sure is. More'n enough, if it was handled right."

"The thing to do then is to make the drive together."

Art Gurney, in the act of taking a drink from the whiskey bottle, glanced at him, startled. "How's that?"

"I said the way to get around all this grass

trouble is for us to make the drive together, combine the herds and all move through the valley at the same time. There'd be nobody getting to the grass first, and there'd be no chance for somebody like Zurcher, or Dave, to pull a raw stunt the way they did last year."

Gurney was grinning broadly. "By dang, that's sure the ticket. Whyn't we think of that afore?" Abruptly he sobered, set the bottle on the table untouched. "Only one thing wrong . . . you'd never get Tom Lindsey and Marie to string along with the idea."

"I don't intend to ask Marie. I'll take it on my own shoulders. Lindsey's the one I'll have to convince."

"Something else. It'll be like riding on a wagon loaded with gunpowder, throwing the two crews together. There's bound to be a pile of trouble."

"We can keep them apart. When's the drive set to go?"

"Gather's 'most done now. I think they're figuring on heading out end of the week."

"Box K's probably ready, too."

"Prob'ly. And trying to get away first . . . same as always."

"It's best I see Lindsey, talk him into the idea."

"Tomorrow. You sure ain't riding back

there tonight," Gurney said bluntly. "You're needing some shut-eye. The shape you're in, you'd not make it to the gate."

"I mean tomorrow, after I've hunted up Zurcher."

"You decided he's the one who rousted you around?"

"I'll know when I talk to him."

"Then what?" Gurney asked in a quiet, tense way. "Aim to square up . . . ?"

XI

Art Gurney rode with him that next morning — to "show him the best way to Willow Creek," the old cowpuncher had put it. Holloway had grinned, accepted the man's offer although he disliked the thought of drawing Art into his personal problems.

But Gurney had been insistent, and shortly after breakfast Jess, stiff, sore, and aching in every bone and muscle, climbed onto the blue roan, and with Gurney beside him on his little paint struck out for the settlement.

After the few hours of restless sleep he had had, he was convinced now the ambush had been the work of Walt Zurcher and his crowd, despite the fact he had no actual proof. Tom Lindsey might employ every

232

means to disrupt the Slash M's operation, but he was not a man who would sink to murder.

It had to be Zurcher. He, alone, stood to spoil the outlaw's plans, and Walt would want him out of the way — permanently. It was that simple. He felt a grimness settle over him as that realization registered fully. But he'd have something to say about it. He'd been up against Walt Zurcher's kind before. And then a thought came to him: *That's the trouble up here . . . everybody's walking around with a grudge. This is different, he told himself. This is a personal thing between Zurcher and me . . . has nothing to do with the feud.* Or did it? Wasn't it all a part, a product of the simmering, about-to-explode war? He was Slash M's foreman — that made him and whatever he did a piece of the whole fabric. If he called out Zurcher, shot him down. . . .

Holloway swore quietly. An arm's length away Art Gurney heard, turned his weathered face to him. "Them cuts paining you right smart, son?" he asked sympathetically.

Jess nodded, letting it go at that. How could he explain to the old cowpuncher his change in attitude, that there was a need for peace, not vengeance — that a deliberately planned shoot-out was not the answer? Art would never understand. But he was not letting Walt Zurcher off entirely. He had to be warned.

"Might be smart to drop in on Doc Peters whilst we're in town," Gurney said. "Some of them cuts is a mite deep."

"That'd be fine," Jess replied.

Willow Creek's single street was almost deserted when they rode in. A half dozen horses stood at the hitch rack in front of the Mulehead Saloon. A buckboard was drawn up before Gholson's General Store. They were the only indications of life.

Holloway angled toward the Mulehead, pulled to a stop next to the other horses. He sat there for a long moment staring at the splintered façade of the squat structure, and then swung stiffly from the roan.

"Reckon they're inside for sure," Gurney commented. "Them's their nags." He eyed the animals critically. "Ain't no ropes hanging from Nemo and Red's saddles. Reckon that ought to prove something to you."

Jess nodded, mounted the step, and crossed to the batwing doors, the old cowpuncher only a stride behind him. He paused there, looking over the top of the doors into the interior of the saloon. A moment later he entered.

Stopping a third of the way to the bar, he

glanced around the room. Zurcher, Nemo, Red, with two men he had never before seen, were sitting at a table in a corner playing cards. They had not looked up, were unaware of his presence.

Immediately Holloway wheeled and crossed to where the men sat. Walt Zurcher's head came up suddenly. Surprise blanked his eyes. Red and Nemo were no less shocked.

"Reckon you sure didn't expect to see him again," Art Gurney drawled in a dry, bantering tone. "Well, you better start. . . ."

Jess lifted his hand, silenced the older man. His level glance locked with that of Zurcher. "You didn't quite get the job done, Walt. I had it in mind to settle up with you for trying, but I'm letting it pass."

Zurcher eased back in his chair. "What the hell you talking about?"

Holloway's jaw tightened. "Don't play dumb with me. I'm giving you a warning. You're finished around here."

"You telling me to move on?"

"If you figure on staying healthy."

"You ain't running me off . . . !" Red shouted, coming half out of his chair.

Holloway reached out quickly. Placing his hand, palm forward, against the redhead's face, he shoved him back down.

"Don't push your luck," he murmured softly. "I'm not sure I like what I'm doing."

Zurcher shook his head. "You blaming us for that deal last night?"

"What deal?"

The outlaw realized his error, caught himself, stirred uneasily. "Well, whatever's sticking in your craw . . . could've been somebody else who done it. . . ."

"Done what?" Jess pressed.

"God damn it, done whatever you're crawling on us for!"

"Could've been some of the Box K boys," Red suggested, trying to be of help to the floundering Zurcher.

Holloway gave them a taut smile. "That's what you'd like for me to believe . . . only I know better."

"How . . . ?" Red began, and then hushed instantly as Walt Zurcher flashed him a warning look.

"It's not important how," Jess said, the same tight grin on his lips. "You made your try and it didn't work. Next time something happens, I'll look you up and it won't be to talk."

"You ain't scaring me off," Zurcher said. "A man's got a right to do his own choosing."

"Going to be risky for you. I'll stand for

no more trouble."

"You blaming me for this ruckus between the Morrels and the Lindseys?"

"Not for starting it . . . for keeping it going and making it worse."

Zurcher shrugged. "Better be telling Dave Morrel to move on, too."

"I'll handle him my way. Right now I'm talking to you."

"And maybe I ain't listening so good."

"It's up to you. I aim to keep things from getting any worse around here, and you're the spark that could set it off."

Walt picked up his cards, toyed with them. "You sound like some tin-star marshal. How much time you giving us, Mister Lawman?"

Holloway clung to his temper. "The day's young. Just keep remembering that it'll be you who'll do the dying."

The outlaw stiffened. "Maybe," he said quietly.

Jess nodded curtly and wheeled around. Eyes on the mirror of the backbar, he crossed to the doors, closely followed by Gurney.

Reaching the batwings, he paused. Neither Zurcher nor any of the others at the table, aware of his surveillance, had stirred.

"That's the way it will be from here on,"

he said over his shoulder. "I'll be watching every move you make."

XII

Holloway stepped out onto the gallery of the Mulehead, stopped. Art Gurney moved up beside him. The old cowpuncher was silent, disappointed in the encounter; he had expected a showdown — a killing, Jess realized, and now was having his doubts. He faced the grizzled oldster.

"Not the way you figured I'd handle it?"

Gurney wagged his head. "Speaking plain, it ain't. You ought've called Zurcher out, settled things with him once and for all. That was what Saul would have wanted."

"Maybe. Right now killing's not the answer here."

"There'll be a few who'll say you backed down. . . ."

"Their privilege," Jess said disinterestedly. "There's always a lot of people anxious for a fight . . . as long as they're not in it."

Art made no comment, only stared off into the street. Inside the saloon Walt Zurcher laughed.

"Reckon he figures he come out on top," Gurney said. "And he'll be telling every man that walks through them doors so."

"Let him," Holloway snapped. "He knows better. I don't aim to turn a family squabble into a first-class range war unless I'm forced to. I'm heading out to see Lindsey . . . to talk."

"No call to make the ride," the old cowpuncher said, pointing toward the far end of the settlement. "That's him and his missus coming now."

Jess swung about. The rancher and his wife, in a light buggy, were slanting for Gholson's. He remained motionless until Lindsey had pulled up to the rack in front of the store, then stepped off into the dust and crossed over.

He touched the brim of his hat in a courteous greeting to the woman, nodded to Lindsey. "I was on my way over to talk with you."

The rancher, in the act of wrapping the reins about the whipstock, did not look up. "Don't know as we've got anything to chaw on."

"Wrong there. If we don't get a few things settled pretty quick, it'll be too late."

Lindsey stiffened. "That a threat?"

"No. More like a promise. If things keep piling up the way they are, someday we're going to have a mighty bad explosion."

"What did you want to talk about, Mister

239

Holloway," the rancher's wife asked, leaning forward.

Lindsey jerked around, giving her a sharp look. She only smiled, continued to study Jess.

"The cattle drive. I did some asking and found out how all this trouble got started. . . ."

"It wasn't Box K that got it going!" Tom Lindsey broke in angrily.

"It doesn't matter now who it was. The thing to do is call a halt."

"Just like that, eh?" Lindsey said, snapping his fingers. "You're a fool, Holloway, if you think a little jabbering's going to wipe out all the. . . ."

"I don't expect it to," Jess cut in, "but I expect you to be man enough to try and end it. And you're smart enough to know it'll come to bloodshed one of these days."

The rancher's jaw tightened. "When it does, I reckon we can take care of ourselves."

"The point I'm getting at is that there's no call for it to go that far."

"Up to you and the Morrels."

A short, balding man wearing a bib apron appeared in the doorway of the store, leaned against the frame. Gholson, apparently, was taking it all in.

"What was it you wanted to say about the drive?" Mrs. Lindsey prompted.

Instantly the rancher whirled on her. "Stay out of this, Hannah!"

Hannah Lindsey squared her shoulders, thrust her chin forward. "I won't stay out of it! Lot of foolishness, every bit of it. Go ahead, Mister Holloway."

"I figure we ought to throw the herds together and make one drive to Springer."

"What was that?" Lindsey demanded in an incredulous voice.

"It seems there's always been trouble over trail grass. First herd across never leaves much for the one that follows. And there's been some meanness mixed up in it, too."

"Like burning it off. . . ."

Jess nodded. "There's plenty of grass for all if it's handled right."

"And you figure running the two herds together'll fix all that?"

"It will. There'll be no more of this first man there gets the gravy while the second man gets the leftovers. That's been the bone of contention at the bottom of everything."

Tom Lindsey stared at Holloway, smiled. "Now, you wouldn't've hatched out this little scheme after you found out my herd's ready to move and Morrel's ain't, would you?"

Jess shook his head. "I didn't know where you stood, and I think the Slash M beef is ready, or just about."

The rancher studied the backs of his hands. After a moment he shrugged. "It's some kind of a trick. . . ."

"No trick. And I'm not asking you to turn your stock over to me or anything like that. We'll each run our own crews, take separate chuck wagons if you say. And we'll both go along. It'll be just like any drive except we'll move out together."

Again Lindsey was silent for a time. Then: "Heard you'd fired them hardcases that's been hanging around Morrels'. That true?"

"It's true. They've been warned to move on."

"Don't mean they will."

Holloway stirred, dismissed the statement. "What about it? You agreeable to make the drive together?"

"Did you talk this over with the Morrels?" Lindsey countered, his eyes reaching beyond Holloway.

Jess said: "Not necessary. Except they'll see it my way."

"Now's a good time to find out," Lindsey replied. "Here comes Dave."

Holloway turned, watched Morrel head in toward the rack fronting the Mulehead. He noticed then that several men had gathered on the saloon's porch and were listening to the discussion taking place between Lindsey and himself. In the forefront were Walt Zurcher and Red. Elsewhere he could see Nemo and the two strangers who had been at the table.

Dave dismounted, wrapped his reins around the pole. Zurcher stepped up to him, spoke briefly, and fell back. Immediately Morrel wheeled, crossed the street, and confronted Holloway.

"What's this talk about making a drive with Lindsey?"

"It's what I plan to do if he's agreeable."

"The hell you will!" Dave snapped. "The time'll never come when you'll see Slash M stock walking with Box K stuff!"

"It's here now," Jess said calmly. "Now go on over and play with your friends. This is none of your business."

Dave Morrel flushed hotly. "My stock . . . by God, I got a right . . . !"

"You gave up your rights when you started running with Walt Zurcher," Holloway said. "Move on!"

Tom Lindsey laughed. Dave threw him a furious glance, spun on his heel, and returned to where Zurcher and the others stood. Not pausing, he mounted the step and entered the saloon. After a moment, the outlaw, trailed by his friends, followed. Jess waited until all were inside, and then, raw with impatience, weary of the endless bickering, turned to the rancher.

"What about it? Let's get this settled."

Lindsey rubbed at his chin. "Got to do some studying. Ain't so sure. . . ."

"Well, I am," Hannah Lindsey declared in a firm voice. "This thing has gone far enough. I want it stopped, and it seems to me Mister Holloway has the right idea."

"Now, wait a minute . . . ," Lindsey began.

"No, you wait. Marie Morrel and I were friends for a long time but this argument between you and Saul broke it up, and friends and neighbors aren't so plentiful that you can spare even one. Besides, as he said, it's going to end up in bloodshed if we don't stop it. What do you want us to do, Mister Holloway?"

"Call me Jess for one thing, ma'am," Holloway said, breaking the tension. "Then next I reckon we ought to decide on a place to gather the herds."

"Crater Cañon'd be the best," Art Gurney, silent through it all, suggested. "You think so, Tom?"

"Be the best," the rancher said slowly. "When?"

Jess glanced at Gurney. The old cow-puncher spat. "Slash M stuff's ready, or almost. I figure was we to start pushing hard today, we could be in the cañon tomorrow. Drive could begin next morning."

"That'll be Saturday. Move out at sunup," Jess said. He stepped forward, extended his hand to Lindsey. "There'll be nobody sorry for this. You've got my word."

The rancher nodded. "Probably something we should've thought of years ago. But I reckon I'd never've got around to believing it if this here wife of mine hadn't done some pushing."

Jess smiled at Hannah Lindsey, expressing his gratitude, and wheeled to cross to the roan. He had a glimpse of Red moving through the batwings of the Mulehead, going into the saloon — knew immediately what it meant.

Dave, or Walt Zurcher, had sent him back to listen, to see if Lindsey would agree to the proposal. They would know now that he had. They would be aware, too, of the location of the gather and the hour of the drive's beginning.

XIII

"Trouble brewing, sure'n hell," Gurney muttered, eyes on the saloon doors. "Knowed you should've cut Walt Zurcher's water off right when you had the chance."

Jess slanted a look at the old cowpuncher. "Only a dead man's a good man, that it?"

"Depends. If you're talking about the likes of Zurcher and his bunch, I'm agreeing."

Holloway was silent for a few moments. "You ever kill a man?"

Gurney hawked, spat. "Can't say as I have."

"Didn't think so. Makes a big difference," Jess said, and moved on to where the roan gelding waited.

They mounted, headed north out of the settlement for Morrels'. Holloway was feeling better about the situation — thanks to Hannah Lindsey. While there had been a strong possibility Tom would have eventually given his approval of the plan, she had forced him to make an immediate decision. And the drive, if successful, would be a long stride toward peace.

"You still aim to keep this from Marie?" Gurney asked as they broke from the last of the houses and veered west into the cedar-studded hills.

"Not much chance of that now. Dave'll break his neck to tell her."

Art grunted. "You can bet on it. He sure was put out . . . Lindsey laughing at him the way he did."

"It was rough on him."

"He had it coming. About time Dave started doing and thinking right. It'll take a few hard jolts like that one to make him see it. You figure Marie'll try to stop the drive?"

"She's got as much to gain as the Lindseys."

"But supposing she bows her neck?"

"I'll give her the same choice as I did when I ran off Zurcher. Either I'm the foreman . . . or she fires me."

The old cowpuncher chuckled. "Sort of got her there. She promised Saul she'd let you take care of things. She ain't one to go back on her word."

Gurney paused, looked over his shoulder. The road had reached the beginning of the higher, brush-covered hills and was beginning to wind its way toward a distant line of ragged buttes. Jess glanced at the older man.

"Something bothering you?"

"Got myself an uneasy feeling," Gurney replied, shrugging. "I figure we ain't heard the last of Zurcher and his bunch yet."

"Not much they can do but talk Dave into

trying to stop the drive through his ma."

"They could put a bullet in your head," Gurney said flatly. "You don't know them skunks like I do."

"I'll be keeping my eye. . . ."

"I knowed it!" the old cowpuncher interrupted. "We're being trailed!"

Jess turned quickly. He caught a fleeting glimpse of several riders in the distance. All seemed to be hugging the edge of the trail as though trying to keep out of sight.

"Don't slow down," he said. "Let them think we don't know they're there. You figure it's Zurcher?"

"Who else? Ain't likely to find pilgrims on this road."

It could be Walt Zurcher — Zurcher and Dave with Nemo and Red and possibly also the two strangers he had seen in the saloon. Jess gave the reason for their pursuit careful thought.

They could have only one idea in mind — prevent him and Art Gurney from reaching the ranch and getting the drive under way. Success — and the healing of the breach between the two ranches — depended on getting Slash M cattle to Crater Cañon on time and being ready to begin the drive. Lindsey would consider a failure to do so as an indication that the truce was over. Dave and Zurcher would again have everything their way and the simmering trouble would resume its climb to an inevitable, bloody explosion.

He looked back over the long slope. He could see none of the riders at the moment as brush hid them from view. Abruptly he swung off the trail and cut in behind squat piñon trees. Gurney wheeled in beside him.

"What's up?"

"I've got to know for sure it's Zurcher."

"It's him," the old cowpuncher said with conviction.

Holloway made no answer, began to angle across the slope for a shoulder of rock jutting from the hillside. If it proved to be someone else, all well and good; they could continue on their way to the Slash M and get preparations started for the drive. But if it were the outlaws — and Dave Morrel — he would have to take steps to head them off, turn them back.

Reaching the bulging fault, he dismounted and moved to its extreme edge. Searching the slope below, he finally located the trail, fixed his gaze upon an open stretch lying between two clumps of brush. The riders would be fairly close — dangerously so — when they crossed the opening, but Jess Holloway felt he had to know for certain the identities of the men.

The moments dragged, became minutes. Art Gurney stirred restlessly. "Ought to be moving. Going to push us plenty getting the herd to the cañon on time. Chuck wagon's got to be loaded. Remuda lined up. All the boys told."

"Five minutes won't make any difference," Jess said. "The thing we've got to know is whether we can expect trouble from Zurcher or not."

Gurney bobbed his head. "Just figure on it. Walt and Dave'll cook up plenty."

Jeff straightened. Two men had ridden into the cleared area. Their horses were moving at a fast walk while they held themselves high on the saddle, staring upslope. A moment later three others came into view a bit to their left; another appeared on the right.

"Zurcher and Dave, sure enough," Jess murmured, his eyes on the two men in the lead. "Got Red and Nemo . . . and that pair we saw in the saloon . . . with them."

"Six. Regular little army," Gurney said. "Walt sure's aiming to just take over."

Holloway crossed to the roan and went to the saddle. He knew now what to expect — trouble in plentiful quantities.

"How many men can we spare for the drive?" Gurney asked. "Six, eight . . . ?"

"Six, including you, ought to be enough," Jess said. "I don't want to strip the ranch. Listen close, Art. Head for the Slash M. Get there fast without letting Zurcher or any of his bunch see you. Pick the riders you want and have them get the herd moving toward the cañon. I'm leaving it up to you to get everything set."

Gurney nodded, frowned. "What'll you be doing?"

"Waiting for Zurcher. I've got to keep him busy."

The lines in the old cowpuncher's face deepened. "What good'll that do?"

"If I can keep that bunch tied down for the day, you won't have any problems getting the stock to the cañon in time."

Gurney nodded as understanding came to him. "For a fact! You're the bait that draws off the wolves whilst I move the stock." He sobered. "Ain't so sure that's smart. They's six of them to your one."

"I can handle them. The main thing is for you to get the herd there and ready to head out Saturday morning with Lindsey."

"What'll I tell Marie?"

"Nothing. Don't let her know what you're up to."

"Maybe she'll get wise anyway."

"Then tell her to see me. Say you've got

your orders and you're carrying them out."

Gurney started to wheel away, checked himself. His features were serious. "Watch yourself, son. Don't go taking no big chances."

"Never was much a hand at that," Jess assured him. "Just you see we're ready for that drive!"

XIV

Holloway waited until Art Gurney had disappeared into the brush and then doubled back to the trail. Walt Zurcher and his men would be near, he realized, and he was cutting matters a bit thin, but it had to be done.

Reaching the roadway, he pulled into its center, halted, taking care not to look downslope; he was gambling on still being beyond pistol range of the outlaws.

From the tail of his eye he saw distant motion. It was only a flash as one of the riders moved into view and then instantly dodged behind some brush. Jess grinned tightly and turned up the trail. The bait, as Gurney had termed him, had been offered.

He rode at a set pace designed to give the old cowpuncher as great a lead as possible while not allowing Zurcher to pull in too close. He looked ahead. The buttes were no more than a half mile distant. He would make a stand there, he decided, well up in the rocks where he could have a good sweep of the slope below.

He reached the first outcrop of loose shale and boulders. The trail veered left and he cut away, pointing directly toward a deep slash in the face of the nearest butte that would permit him to gain the crest. The roan began to blow as the footing became more difficult. Drawing his rifle, Jess dismounted, moved out, leading the gelding.

They reached the ravine, narrow and filled with feathery Apache plume and sharp-pointed yucca. They started the climb. The roan snorted and heaved as the shale and storm-washed gravel skidded from under his hoofs, but he managed to stay upright. Finally they reached a narrow level and halted.

Holloway glanced around. They were just below the summit now, within easy reach. He could see Zurcher and the others, absently counted them — six men. They still followed the main trail, apparently unaware yet that he had veered off. That was good. It was important the outlaws think he and Gurney were still together and headed for the Slash M.

Leaning the rifle against a rock, Jess led

the roan the balance of the way to the crest, stationed him out of sight in a hollow below the rim, and then returned to the ledge. Taking up the long gun, he checked the magazine, assured himself that it was full, and laid it upon a flat slab of sandstone at the end of the shelf. Drawing his pistol, he retraced his steps and took up a position at the opposite point. That done, he settled down to wait. He was ready.

Dave Morrel and Zurcher came into view first. They rode side-by-side on the trail, both craning their necks as they looked ahead. Their horses now moved at a faster gait indicating that the rough area of the buttes had evidently been selected as the place where they intended to close in on the two men they thought were still in front of them.

A few lengths to the left the four other men, now in a single group, made their appearance. They were abreast, and Red seemed to be holding their attention with something he was telling — a story perhaps, or a joke.

Holloway cocked his pistol, and hunched low, moved to the front of the rocky shelf. The range was too great for a handgun, but he was less interested at the moment in hitting one of them than he was in bringing the party to a halt. Taking general aim at Zurcher, he thumbed two quick shots.

Whirling quickly, and still low, he ran to the far end of the ledge, seized the rifle, and levered another shot at the remaining men.

Raising his head, he looked to see what the effect had been. Zurcher and Morrel had dismounted and sought safety behind a pile of boulders to the right of the trail. Red and the others were also off their saddles and were legging it for a brush-choked arroyo a half dozen strides below them. Jess snapped a second bullet at them to speed them on their way. The distance was not too far for the rifle and dust spurted about their heels.

Satisfied that he had made his presence known and established the belief that both he and Gurney were entrenched in the higher rocks of the slope, Holloway returned to his original position. He had them neatly pinned down. The next move was up to them.

It was not long in coming. Red leaped suddenly from the ravine in which he and the three others had taken refuge, sprinted awkwardly across the uneven ground for the rocks where Dave and Walt Zurcher lay. Jess snapped a shot at him with his six-gun, then hurried to the rifle.

Instantly the men below opened up. They could not see him, he knew, and were angrily returning his fire in a burst of exasperation. All were using pistols, having left their rifles on the horses. Holloway turned his attention to that bit of neglected business; it would be stupid to allow the outlaws to improve their predicament in any way.

Aiming at the earth in front of the horses, now clustered in a small circle, he levered three hurried shots. The animals reared in fright, wheeled, galloped off down the slope for a considerable distance. The long guns were now well beyond the outlaws' reach.

A fresh burst of shooting erupted in the wake of this, but the bullets all fell short, *thudding* into the loose gravel and rocks below the ledge. Holloway continued to peer over the edge; it would be smart to impress Zurcher and his followers even more of the fact that they were thoroughly covered.

Again it was the redhead. Jess saw him burst from behind the rocks that shielded Dave Morrel and Zurcher, start for the ravine. Holloway permitted him to get halfway, then, taking careful aim, placed a bullet at his feet.

Red yelled, stumbled, went sprawling full

length into the dirt. He gathered himself instantly, began to crawl frantically for the wash. Wasting no more of the rifle's cartridges, Jess threw a revolver shot at the man — more for the benefit of sound than anything else.

With Red again in the arroyo and out of sight, Holloway settled back. He glanced at the sun. It was well onto noon, and, cupped in the rocks as he was, the heat was beginning to make itself felt. He thought of his canteen, swore softly at his shortsightedness; it was on his saddle and to obtain it he would have to expose himself. While there was no danger from the weapons of the men below, he was reluctant to reveal his exact position.

The day wore on. Thirst began to plague him insistently and he again cursed himself for his neglect. It was the one error in a perfectly executed plan. But he refused to let discomfort bother him too much. There had been occasions when he had gone longer without water, and survived. He had only to wait until darkness fell.

Around 3:00 Dave Morrel made a try for the horses. Jess drove him back with two closely placed shots. As the young rancher dived headlong into the protection of the rocks, the other men began to fire. Holloway sat back, grinned at their futile efforts. He could imagine their fury.

An hour later the shooting, for no apparent reason that he could tell, broke out again. Suspicious, he changed positions, his eyes probing the brush below the rocks where Morrel and Zurcher lay, and along the wash in which the others had taken cover. He could see no movement.

Gravel rattled hollowly off to his left. He wheeled swiftly, threw his glance along the steep face of the butte. He could see no one, but a small puff of dust was hanging lazily at the foot of the grade.

Instantly he crossed to the end of the ledge, eyes on the welter of loose rock and brushy growth at the base of the butte. A stone *clicked* — Jess strained to place the slight noise. It seemed to have come from higher up on the butte — almost parallel to his position.

Abruptly a gun roared, shattering the hush. Dust showered Holloway as the bullet dug into the sun-baked wall behind him. He ducked low, hurriedly tried to locate the marksman.

A second shot came. He saw the bulge of blue-white smoke, the hasty withdrawal of a man's arm as he jerked back behind a jutting of rock farther along the face of the butte.

He realized what had happened. He had figured the arroyo in which Red and the others lay ended when it reached the foot of the formation; instead, it probably carved its way to the right, possibly connected with a second ravine. By following it out and making use of distractions afforded by his companions, one of the party had managed to climb the butte.

Grim, Holloway pulled back, placing the vertical ridge between himself and the outlaw. He looked downslope, immediately threw his rifle to his shoulder. Zurcher and Dave had taken advantage of the unguarded moments, had left the pile of rocks and reached the horses. As he lowered the weapon, aware of the distance, he saw them mount, draw their own rifles from the boot.

He glanced again at the sun. Too early to pull out — Art Gurney would need until dark. He would have to continue stalling Walt Zurcher and his men. But he could not do it here — not with one man on the face of the butte who could get in a lucky shot. And now Dave and Zurcher had rifles. If he remained, he could become trapped, pinned down.

Whirling, he ducked low and raced up the

narrow opening in the rocks for the crest. Bullets screamed against the hard surfaces around him, screamed off into space as Morrel and Zurcher brought their guns into use. He plunged on, gained the top, and flung himself over the rim. Not hesitating, he ran to where the roan was picketed, jerked the reins loose, and vaulted onto the saddle. Spinning the blue about, he headed for a place on the rim of the butte beyond where he figured the one outlaw was stationed.

He came out barely fifty feet below the man. He was one of the pair that had been in the saloon. Dropping from the saddle, Jess made his way to the edge of the butte. He could see Red, Nemo, and the third man. They were below, standing upright in the arroyo, their eyes on the ledge where he had been. Farther over, Morrel and Walt Zurcher, again on foot, were advancing slowly up the grade, rifles poised. Apparently they thought him still to be in the rocks, on the face of the butte. Steadying himself, he took close aim at the rocks just above the man's head. He pressed off a shot. Dust and rock chips erupted around the outlaw's head. He yelled, jerked away. His feet lost their perch and he fell, dropping a short distance to the slope, and then

260

sliding and rolling the remainder of the way to the bottom.

At the report of Holloway's rifle, Morrel and Zurcher spun. Instantly both began to shoot. With dirt spurting about his boots, Jess hurried to the roan, again leaped to the saddle, and whirled away.

Daring their bullets, he kept himself in full view. He had to keep them at his heels.

XV

He could hear Red shouting about the horses, the words only partly reaching him between the echoing gunshots. The level surface of the rim fell away into a deep swale. The roan dipped over the edge, fighting to retain his footing, and they dropped below the reach of the outlaws' bullets.

Jess pulled to a halt. Dismounting, he went to his belly and crawled to the edge. Morrel and Zurcher, astride their horses, were moving up fast along the foot of the buttes. Their intentions were clear; they hoped to cut him off farther on.

Beyond them, Red and Nemo, their mounts recovered, were swinging to the saddle. One of the strangers was assisting the other onto his horse. Apparently he had been injured in the fall from the butte. As

Jess watched, he turned, headed back in the direction of town while his friend hurried to catch up with Red and Nemo, now spurring to overtake Zurcher and Morrel.

Satisfied, Holloway returned to the roan and mounted. He stared ahead, wondering as to the nature of the country. It appeared to be a continuing roll of low, brush-covered hills and smaller buttes. Touching the gelding with his spurs, he moved on.

He would lead them north, playing a grim game of hide-and-seek in the rough badland until sunset. Then he would shake them off and double back to the Slash M. By that hour it would be too late for the outlaws to carry out their plans.

He crossed before them a short time after that, offering himself as a fleeting target to the five men. All were moving now in a compact group.

They opened up on him immediately. He gave them two answering shots and spurred on, pointing for a low, brush-filled swale a half mile distant. He reached the edge of the hollow, paused to look back. Zurcher, followed closely by Red, Nemo, and the tall newcomer, were pulling out of the valley, streaming across a narrow flat.

Where was Dave Morrel?

That question set up a quick worry within

him as he sent the roan loping toward the brush. Had he deserted the party, turned for the ranch?

He shrugged away all thoughts of young Morrel. It was Zurcher and his crowd that presented the greater danger; best he concentrate on them. Later he would meet and handle any problem Dave might create.

His appearance at the edge of the brushy swale immediately brought a flurry of gunshots, most of which fell considerably short. Drawing his rifle, he scattered the men with two bullets, and then plunged into the tangle of rank growth.

At once he was lost to view, as was his sight of them. He swung right, began to cut back toward the buttes. A half mile later a rise lifted before him and he struck for it. Halting on the summit, he looked for the outlaws. They were almost directly below him and, having missed his turn off, were moving straight on.

He remained there, finding time at last to satisfy his thirst from his canteen. When the outlaws were finally lost to him in the undergrowth, he came about, retraced his path, intending to get below them. If his hunch were right, Zurcher, not finding him before them, would cut back to the buttes where he could get a better view of the surrounding land.

Jess moved on, allowing the blue to pick his way in and out of the scrub cedars and thick rabbitbrush. He glanced again to the sun. It was lowering fast. It wouldn't be necessary to maintain the game much longer.

Abruptly the dry scrape of leather against brush, the grunt of a horse, came to him. He pulled up sharp, alarm racing through him. Before he could wheel away, the rider broke into view only paces to his right.

It was Nemo! The gunman's eyes flared with surprise. His hand darted toward the pistol on his hip. Holloway drew fast, fired without aiming. Nemo's mount reared at the sound, shied off.

From somewhere behind the dark gunman shouts went up. Anger at his own carelessness ripped through Jess. He had been so cocksure of what Zurcher would do — and he had blundered straight into them.

He whirled the roan about, snapping a second bullet at Nemo, another into the general direction of the shouting, and spurred the gelding into a reckless gallop for the buttes.

"Head him off!"

It was Walt Zurcher's voice coming from the left.

"He's making for the buttes!"

He recognized Red's tones, bent lower over the roan's arched neck. They were close — too close. He looked about, tried to choose a denser area into which he might flee. It was not there. The nearer he drew to the cliffs the more sparse the growth became.

Holloway reacted from instinct. He turned the blue hard right, cut sharply into the last of the thick underbrush. He spurred the horse cruelly, taking his chances on him stumbling for a good ten yards, then hauled him to a quick stop.

Drawing his pistol, he punched out the empty cartridges, reloaded — and waited. If the outlaws missed his turn, they would continue on toward the crest and he would have no use for the weapon. If they had not been fooled — he would have to shoot it out.

He heard them a moment later, their horses moving at a fast walk. Zurcher's voice was sharp, angry.

"Keep strung out. He ain't going no place, once he gets to the top. We'll box him in."

"Could make a run, either direction," Red said.

"What do you want . . . somebody holding him for you?"

"Just saying it'll be no cinch. . . ."

"It will be if you're watching what you're doing. We'd've had him right now if Nemo hadn't been half asleep."

"God damned horse," the gunman protested. "Started pitchin'. Couldn't get off a shot."

Zurcher made some reply but the words were lost to Holloway as the riders passed on. He slid his weapon into the holster, sighed, and swung around. There was no need to bother any longer with Walt Zurcher and his crew; by the time they discovered that he was not trapped against the buttes, it would be dark.

He cut across the low hills, taking the precaution to remain in the brush, until he was again on the mesa above the ledge where he had made his stand. He crossed over, made a junction with the trail, and curved west.

With the shadows lengthening and growing darker around him, he put the gelding to a comfortable lope and headed for the Slash M.

Everything should be ready by that hour — or nearly so, he felt — and failing as he had, Walt Zurcher would likely give it up. The drive should get under way with no problems. He wondered if Dave had been able to stir up any amount of trouble for Gurney and decided that it was unlikely. Matters would have been too far along for him to prove a hindrance.

He topped a hill, saw the lights of the ranch glowing through the darkness far below. He realized then how tired he was — and hungry. He'd check with Art Gurney as soon as he rode in, assure himself that all was in readiness, then he would have a bite of supper and pile into bed. He wanted to be in good shape when the drive began.

He passed under the gate heading, pulled the gelding to a walk. No use arousing Marie Morrel. It would just mean an argument — and he was too beat for that.

Reaching the main house, he circled by it, moved on to his quarters. A shadow detached itself from the blackness along the bunkhouse. In the pale moonlight he recognized Dave. A pistol glinted in the boy's hand.

"Climb down!" Morrel ordered, grasping the roan's head stall. "You're calling off the cattle drive."

XVI

Jess Holloway made no move to comply. Slumped on the saddle, he studied Morrel's taut, angry face. Apparently he had figured it right. Dave had arrived too late to do anything about the herd and was now playing his last, desperate card.

"Forget it," he said quietly. "The drive heads out in the morning."

"The hell it does!" Dave shouted, waving the pistol threateningly. "I'm giving you an order, and you're taking it!"

Holloway shook his head. "I don't take orders from you, gun or no gun. Might as well put it away."

Fury overwhelmed Dave Morrel. He lunged, seized Jess by the arm, attempting to drag him from the saddle. Holloway slipped sideways, caught the horn as he came off. He kicked free of the stirrups, struck hard on one heel. Instantly Morrel crowded against him, clubbing with his pistol. Jess took a glancing blow on the side of the head. There was little pain but it sent his own anger soaring.

He caught Dave by the wrist, spun him half around, slammed a knotted fist into his belly. The younger man gasped, struck out wildly. Holloway ducked the blow, slapped Morrel hard across the face. Dave staggered back, dropped his revolver. Holloway, thoroughly aroused, kicked it off into the darkness, shoved Morrel against the bunkhouse wall, and started another blow.

"That will be enough!"

Marie Morrel's sharp, precisely pronounced words cut the half darkness like a knife. Holloway stepped back, chest heaving, turned to face her.

She stepped to Morrel's side. He sagged against the building, head slung forward, one hand pressed to his middle as he fought to recover his wind.

"Dave . . . are you all right?" she asked, touching his shoulder.

He jerked away savagely. "Leave me be!"

Marie frowned, stared at him for a moment, and shifted her attention to Holloway. "What's this all about?"

Jess shrugged. "A little misunderstanding."

"Misunderstanding hell!" Dave grated. "Ask him what he's doing with our cattle."

"The cattle?" she echoed. "What about them?"

"A better question would be to ask him what he's been doing all day," Jess replied coolly.

Marie shook her head impatiently. "I don't know what's going on here, but I intend to find out. And I don't want questions. I want answers. You, Holloway, what about the herd?"

"He's throwing it in with Lindsey's, that's what!" Dave said before Jess could reply.

"Throwing in? What's that mean?"

"It means instead of fighting with him over trail grass and maybe running ten pounds of meat off every steer we've got, we'll move the stock out together in one big herd."

Marie Morrel's eyes opened with surprise, filled quickly with hostility. "You'd dare do that without my permission?" she demanded in a low voice.

"I figured there was no point in asking. You'd be dead set against it, so I went ahead. The herd's in Crater Cañon right now, with Lindsey's stock, waiting for daylight."

"What makes you think you can trust Tom Lindsey?"

"He trusts me, and that's good enough as far as I'm concerned. Anyway, what difference does it make? I'll be there, using our own drovers. Lindsey'll have his. And the cattle sure won't mind walking together. . . ."

"It won't work, Ma!" Dave broke in. "You know that. Lindsey's got some kind of a trick up his sleeve. The only reason he agreed. . . ."

"Lindsey will live up to his bargain if we

stand by ours," Holloway said. "That's the reason I had to keep you and your friends pinned down in the buttes today. I couldn't let you interfere."

Marie turned to Dave. "Pinned down?" she repeated questioningly.

"He held a rifle on us. . . ."

"Us?"

"Walt . . . and Red and Nemo, a couple others."

"Tell it straight, or I will," Jess said, a note of warning in his tone. "I figure she'd like to know why you wanted to stop Art Gurney and me . . . with bullets . . . so we couldn't get the herd to Crater Cañon in time to meet Lindsey."

"You tell her," Dave snapped. "You've got a good start."

"Go ahead," Marie said, looking at Jess. "I think I'd rather hear it from you."

"There's not much else. We saw them following us, after we'd set the deal up with Lindsey. I sent Gurney on to get things started while I kept Dave and his friends busy. We had to get the Slash M stock to the cañon in time or Lindsey'd figure we'd changed our minds, and then we'd be right back with the same old problems . . . worse maybe."

Marie Morrel was quiet for a full minute.

Finally she looked at Holloway. "You think moving the herds together will . . . will end the trouble?"

"It's a step in the right direction. It shouldn't be too hard to iron out whatever else is causing the quarrel."

She nodded. "I guess it's worth any risk."

"Not in my book!" Dave exploded abruptly, stepping away from the wall. He leaned over, scooped up his pistol, and jammed it into his holster. "I won't have nothing to do with it, and you're a fool if you do, Ma!"

Wheeling, he headed toward the main house, walking in quick, angry steps. Moments later hoof beats sounded through the hush.

Marie remained silent until the drumming had faded entirely, and then she faced Jess. "Your idea . . . and it better work," she said curtly, and turned away.

Jess grinned to himself as he watched her leave. She knew he was right and was giving him her stamp of approval. In those moments she reminded him of Saul, of his way of doing things.

He heard the door slam when she entered the house and, sighing, took up the trailing leathers of the roan and led him to the barn. Turning the weary horse over to a sleepy stable boy, he doubled back to his quarters, and stepped inside. A figure sprawled on the bed, snoring deeply.

Jess lit the lamp, looked closer. It was Gurney. The old man sat up, scrubbing at his chin, and gazed about in astonishment.

"Dark, by dang! Must've dropped off whilst I was waiting for you. Just ride in?"

Holloway nodded. The old cowpuncher appeared to be all in; the day's work had been almost too much for him. "Everything ready?"

Gurney yawned, pulled himself to the edge of the bed. "Ready and waiting. Chuck wagon, remuda, the whole shebang."

"How many riders on night hawk?"

"Six. How'd you make out?"

"Had to keep at Zurcher and his crowd until dark. Dave rode off earlier. You see him?"

Gurney wagged his head. "Kept myself clear of the ranch. Didn't want to go bumping into Marie or him, either. Why?"

"Had a few words with them when I got in," Jess said, sinking onto the chair. "Everything's all right with her."

"She's agreeing to the drive with Lindsey?" the old man asked, surprised.

"She is. But not Dave. He just took off in a big hurry for town."

273

"Reckon you know what that means."

Jess nodded, drew his pistol, and checked its loads. "All our men armed?"

"Expect so. They usually are."

"Better be sure before we pull out."

Gurney got to his feet. "You figure Dave and Zurcher'll try stopping the herd?"

Holloway looked up slowly. "I'm sure of only one thing. We've got to make this deal work."

XVII

The morning was gray and cool with a hint of rain to come as Jess Holloway, sided by Gurney, rode into Crater Cañon. The herd, a vast, dark mass strung out in a thick line along its floor, was beginning to stir. Here and there small fires marked the positions of the riders who had spent the night with the cattle, and the two chuck wagons, drawn up at widely separated points, showed signs of life as the cooks began to prepare the early meal.

"Us over to the left," Gurney said, pointing off into the faint, smoky haze.

Jess said — "Meet you there." — and swung to the opposite direction.

He circled the near edge of the herd, noting all were Box K brand, and the thought came to him that the strict isolation of the two ranches was still in effect. It wouldn't hold for long; once the cattle began to move, they would mingle. Perhaps then some of the tension he could feel as he rode toward the Lindsey camp would fade.

The rancher, squatting back against the front wheel of the chuck wagon and nursing a tin cup filled with coffee, glanced up as Holloway swung in and stopped. His face was pinched and drawn, and the early morning sourness of a man too old for the job lay upon him like a blanket.

Jess nodded, said: "Guess we're all set."

Lindsey grunted, motioned indefinitely at the coffee pot suspended above the fire. "Help yourself."

Holloway stepped down. The cook tossed him a cup with total indifference. He caught it, crossed to where the blackened container hung, and under the cool eyes of two Box K riders eating breakfast, poured himself a measure of the steaming liquid.

He grinned at them, returned to where Lindsey sat, and hunkered down close by. "Looks like a fine day coming," he said, attempting to break through the wall of hostility.

Lindsey nodded shortly. "Hope so. Keep your boys in line, Holloway. There's been one scrap already. I won't stand for no hoo-rawin'!"

"I'll look after them," Jess said, faintly angered by the rancher's attitude. "But the sooner you and your hands get that chip off your shoulders. . . ."

"Right where it belongs," Lindsey cut in. "Just you see that Slash M bunch don't try knocking it off."

Anger again stirred Holloway. If you believed Tom Lindsey, it was always the Morrel riders at fault, never a Box K man. Perhaps it was true, considering Dave and Zurcher — but it wasn't reasonable to think Slash M was always in the wrong. He let it pass. No sense in getting off on the wrong foot.

Finishing his coffee, he rose. "Obliged," he said, putting the cup aside. "We'll be ready to move soon as the men eat."

"Better be pretty quick," Lindsey observed. "We're about to get under way."

Holloway stiffened. He was doing his best to hold his temper but Lindsey was pushing hard. "You don't start until I give the signal," he said coldly.

The rancher's face darkened. "Now, wait a damn' minute. . . ."

"No, you wait!" Jess snapped. "The deal we made was that the herds move together.

If you have to hold up a few minutes for me, you'll do it. It'll be the same if you aren't ready. We'll wait. And we stay in one bunch. It won't hurt the cattle to mix. They're all branded."

Lindsey dropped his gaze. After a moment he said: "What's the signal . . . a gunshot?"

Holloway turned to the roan, mounted. "I'll send Art Gurney with word," he said, and pulled away.

He found all of the Slash M cowpunchers at the wagon having breakfast. Accepting a plate from the cook, he moved to where he faced them.

"One thing I want straight with you here and now," he said, claiming their attention. "There'll be no trouble on this drive between you and Lindsey's riders."

"They look for it, they'll get it," a squat, balding man said dryly.

"Not while we're on the trail," Jess snapped. "When it's over, you can do as you damn' well please. That clear?"

"Are we just supposed to set back and let 'em spit in our eye . . . that it?"

"They won't as long as you mind your own business. Now get finished. Time we're moving."

He turned, and, beginning to eat, walked slowly toward the cattle. The herd was up, milling around restlessly. Gurney fell in beside him.

"What'd I tell you? It's going to be like setting on a keg of gunpowder."

"Not if I can stop it. The first man to start something will find himself out of a job on the spot."

"Little rough, ain't it, nailing our boys?"

"The same goes for Lindsey's men. I'll see to it." Holloway paused. "You through eating?"

"Reckon I am."

"Ride over and tell Lindsey we're ready to go. I'll get the boys in the saddle."

The old cowpuncher ambled off. Holloway, having a second thought, called to him: "Tell Lindsey to take the point."

Gurney nodded, continued on toward the picket line. Placing the rancher at the head of the herd away from the dust was only right. The older man would be spared the hard, disagreeable work cowpunchers taking the swing, or side positions, and those at drag, the rear of the cattle, would undergo. Tom Lindsey wasn't as young as he used to be.

An hour later the stock was on the way, flowing out across a broad plain, pointing for the not too distant mouth of the valley where before there had been trouble over the grass.

Jess, circling the herd, checked the positions of his riders, as well as those of the Box K men, found everything to his liking, and forged to the front. Lindsey, on a chunky little black, was well out in the lead. That he was pleased — and relieved — to be riding point was obvious, but he made no mention of it when Holloway swung in beside him.

"I figure to cut straight down the middle of the valley," he said, pointing ahead. "That'll let the cattle spread out, graze along the slopes on both sides."

Jess nodded. "I'm leaving it up to you."

"Ought to reach Rocky Point by dark. Eighteen miles or so. All easy going."

Jess grinned, said: "That'll be fine. You lead the way. I'll see the herd keeps up."

He dropped back, noting the Box K chuck wagon and its trailing remuda off to the side. Morrel's equipment and spare horses were on the far, opposite side of the drive. He shook his head wearily. Maybe, before the trip was over, he could get the two cooks to join forces, establish a common camp.

Three steers darted abruptly from the herd directly ahead of him. A Box K rider yelled, surged forward to haze them back into line. Immediately the steers split — two going one way, the third another. Jess jerked off his hat, swung the roan after the single one as Lindsey's man turned to cut off the pair.

Holloway got his runaway back into the main stream, swerved to give the cowpuncher a hand. Together they drove the two strays into the bawling cavalcade. He started to move on, glanced at the Box K man wiping dust from his eyes.

"Contrary critters!" he shouted.

Lindsey's man grinned, bobbed his head, and Jess rode on.

He saw Ed Floyd a few minutes later, and caught a quick glimpse of the *vaquero,* Gonzales. Neither man saw him, however, and he did not swing from his path to interrupt them.

The herd was staying together well and giving the riders little trouble. It was due partly to the coolness of the weather, Jess realized, and partly because the drive was young. The cattle were rested, in good condition, and not in need of water. Their tempers could change in another day. He hoped the drovers would have changed, too, if such proved to be the fact. A hard to manage herd and a crew of hostile, sore-headed cowpunchers was a combination he did not care to think about.

A light shower fell late in the morning, but it was insufficient to settle the churning dust. By noon a close humidity had set in and man and beast alike were absorbing punishment. It was of short duration, however. As they approached the rock-edged, narrow mouth to the valley, a strong breeze sprang up and immediately the heat was broken.

Jess, riding with Art Gurney, pulled off to one side, watched as the herd slimmed down, and, following Lindsey, began to funnel into the valley.

"Doin' better'n I figured," Gurney said, biting off a corner of his tobacco plug. "Was plumb sure something would've happened by now, couple of the boys tangling, or maybe Dave and Zurcher trying a cute stunt."

"There's still a long way to go," Holloway replied, thinking not of the crew but of Morrel and his friends. "I can't see them letting things slide, not after the way Dave acted last night."

A spatter of gunshots, coming from the valley, sounded above the noise of the herd. Jess threw a quick look at Gurney. The old cowpuncher's jaw was grim.

"Counting our chicks too soon," he said.

Holloway wheeled fast, jammed spurs to the blue, and rushed for the entrance to the valley. Guns were continuing to *crackle,* and, as he dropped off the plain into the broad swale, he saw a dozen or more steers sprawled dead in the dust. The rest of the herd was milling uncertainly, beginning to split into smaller bunches and scatter.

Jess slowed, glanced hurriedly around for signs of the bushwhackers. Through the haze he saw four riders on ahead. There seemed to be more hiding in the rocks along the slopes. At that moment Lindsey, doubled over on his saddle, one hand clamped to his side, appeared through the dust. Ed Floyd was with him. The rancher saw Jess, slanted toward him.

"This why you wanted me out front?" he asked in a dragging voice. "So's I'd be an easy target?"

XVIII

Anger roared through Jess Holloway. "Don't be a damned fool!" he snarled.

Fresh shooting broke out somewhere to their left. Holloway tried to see through the drifting clouds of dust but could determine nothing. He drew his rifle, faced the men.

"Art, get Lindsey over to the chuck wagon

so's he can get fixed up. Ed, I'm leaving the herd to you. Keep the cattle circling. Don't want a stampede on our hands."

"Where you going?" Lindsey demanded.

"Out there," Jess said, pointing in the direction of the gunshots, and spurred away.

"You can't fight them alone . . . !" Gurney yelled after him. There were other words but they were lost in the bawling din of the confused herd.

He rode on, keeping to the fringe of the heaving, darting cattle, eyes sweeping back and forth as he sought to locate the attackers. There were at least two dozen steers down. He saw a rider stretched out on the grass, a broad stain covering his chest. It took only a glance to know that he was dead.

A bitter fury gripped Holloway. This was the work of Dave Morrel — of Zurcher; this was their way of showing him, and all others, that they were in control along the Cimarron. He shook his head. He could understand the workings of Zurcher's mind, and those he had apparently hired to aid in the attack — but Dave Morrel? It was difficult to believe that the son of his old friend Saul could be a party to such a senseless thing.

A rider raced in from the slope to Holloway's right, emptied his revolver into a small jag of steers loping for the hills. Jess brought up his rifle, took quick aim at the man, and fired.

He saw the outlaw wheel and stare at him in surprise, his features unfamiliar, and then suddenly fold and tumble from his saddle.

Immediately Jess cut away, started for the rocks on the hillside. More shooting was coming from that point. He saw a steady run of smoke lifting from behind a clump of cedars, hurriedly poured two shots into the dense shrubbery. The smoke puffs ceased. Moments later a rider burst into the open and started down the grade at a reckless gallop.

Holloway snapped a bullet at him, saw it spurt sand on beyond the laboring horse. The outlaw was too far for a second try. Yells were rising back on the level ground and he wheeled about. Floyd, with three riders, was moving in on the cattle, trying to circle them. Likely the Box K foreman had other men on the opposite side working toward the same purpose but the dust was so thick he could not be sure.

Jess turned, came off the slope, thinking it best to stay in front of the cattle. He caught sight of two riders curving in toward Ed Floyd and the cowpunchers helping him. Riding ahead, he kept his eyes on the pair;

it was impossible to tell if they were outlaws or more of the crew coming to assist the herd.

A moment later he recognized Red. The man with him was another stranger. Instantly Jess slid his rifle into its scabbard, drew his pistol, and sent the roan rushing toward the pair.

"Red!" he shouted, slicing in between the cattle and the two men.

The redhead fired without pausing to aim, apparently recognizing Holloway's voice. Jess squeezed off his shot, saw Red jolt, fall heavily from his horse. He swung to the other outlaw, now veering off. Holloway took close aim at the hunched figure, released his shot. The man straightened suddenly, clawed at his saddle horn, and raced on.

The riders rushed up to him, came to a sliding halt. Gurney! With him were Gonzales, the *vaquero,* and another Box K man.

"Figured you oughtn't be by yourself!" the old cowpuncher shouted.

Jess nodded. "Keep ahead of the herd. Careful who you're shooting at. Dust makes it hard to tell."

"How many out there?" Gurney asked.

"Don't know. Three, maybe four. Zurcher and Nemo for sure."

Gonzales leaned forward, cocked his head. "Also Dave Morrel, eh?"

Jess shrugged. "Could be." He was still finding it difficult to accept.

"If Walt Zurcher's running things, you can bet on it," the Box K cowpuncher said.

Holloway made no comment, simply rode away from the others. They moved in behind him and he waved them aside.

"Spread out. Keep your eyes peeled."

He doubted if Zurcher had given up yet — the outlaw would inflict as much damage as possible, hoping to impress upon all the depth of his ruthlessness. If possible he would stall the drive completely, scatter the cattle. In so doing he would not only prove his point personally, but uphold Dave Morrel's position.

He reached the outer edge of the dust pall, looked around. The slopes of the valley were quite near but he could see no movement among the rocks and brush. Gurney and the others had disappeared and he started to double back when gunshots sounded behind and to his left.

Instantly he wheeled, plunged into the floating curtain of yellow particles. Dimly he could see riders cutting through the cattle but he could not tell if they were drovers or not.

He drew closer, saw Art Gurney, rope in hand, lashing at a small bunch of steers, trying to turn them. Other cowpunchers beyond him were doing the same. Jeff pushed on, reaching the outer, ragged edge of the herd, furious at his inability to locate the source of the shots — and therefore the outlaws. The sounds had been close, or seemed so, but in the swirling noise and confusion, it was difficult to tell.

The gunshots erupted again — hard to his right. He whirled, saw Gonzales and the other Box K man bearing straight for a knot of riders coming from the center of the herd. His nerves tightened. Zurcher and Nemo! He rode ahead, hurried to catch up with Lindsey's men.

Zurcher saw the oncoming riders. The party split, three of them curving to one side, Walt and the little gunman to the other. Holloway grinned wolfishly. Their choice had been to his liking — they were moving toward him.

He veered the roan left in order to meet them head on. The blue was suddenly deep in the herd, fighting to hold his footing among the crowding, shifting steers. It was a dangerous place to be, but Holloway was so engrossed in facing the outlaws that he gave it no thought.

Shooting over to the right told him Gonzales and his partner had come to grips with the rest of Zurcher's crew. He saw Nemo turn, look to that direction, and in that same moment notice him. The gunman shouted something at Zurcher and both men began to turn away, lashing their horses mercilessly as they sought to force a path through the cattle.

Holloway cursed, fearful of losing the pair in the crush. He brought up his pistol to fire, lowered it. There were drovers on beyond the two outlaws. Sawing at the reins, he got the blue turned, felt him tremble as he breasted a solid wall of steers.

Anxiously Jess began to shout, lash out at the cattle as he tried to help the roan. He could barely see Zurcher and Nemo through the haze — and then abruptly he felt the gelding going down under him. He tried to leap clear, but he was hemmed in on all sides.

Holstering his pistol, he jerked off his hat and, still astride the blue, began to slap at the long heads of the steers closing in around him. The blue was fighting to get back on his feet. He made it, partly, went down again as a longhorn crowded against him.

Jess became aware of shouting, and then

of Art Gurney and another rider fighting their way toward him. He lashed out again with his hat, grateful for the fact the cattle were so jammed they scarcely moved.

"*Hi-yah! Hi-yah! Hi'yah-h-h-h!* Dang' jugheads!"

Gurney's rasping voice was close. Jess got himself clear of the blue, stood to one side. Taking the head stall in his hand, he urged the horse to rise. The roan began to struggle again, and then, as Gurney and his helper came in, hazing the stock across to create a small island, he pulled himself upright.

Holloway leaped onto the saddle, turned his eyes in the direction where he had last seen Zurcher and Nemo. There was no sign of them. He sat back, swore deeply. He became aware of Gurney's hoarse voice.

"What in tarnation you doin' here . . . middle of the herd? Aiming to get yourself tromped?"

"Zurcher!" Jess yelled back. "Him and Nemo. About had them when my horse went down."

The old cowpuncher raised himself in his stirrups, glanced around. "Where'd they go?"

Jess shook his head. The cowpuncher with Gurney said: "There was four riders lining

289

out across the slope for town a few minutes ago."

Holloway came to attention. That would be Walt and Nemo — and what was left of his bunch. Zurcher had pulled out, convinced he had accomplished his purpose, that he was still master south of the Cimarron.

But Walt Zurcher was wrong, Jess thought grimly, and, if there was to be peace, he would have to be driven from the country. Holloway recalled his earlier decision to avoid violence, not to create bloodshed. It was too late for that now. There were dead men in the valley; Tom Lindsey and possibly others had been wounded. Zurcher — and Dave Morrel — had laid down the challenge. It was up to him — to accept it — not in vengeance but as a means for bringing it all to an end.

Holloway swung the roan about, started for the slope.

"You going after them?" Gurney yelled.

Jess nodded. "Get the herd moving for Springer. I'll be back."

XIX

He rode into Willow Creek knowing he was expected. Zurcher would have planned it that way.

Halting in front of the clapboard church at the end of the street, he looked ahead. The walks were deserted and there were no horses at any of the hitch racks. Checking his pistol, he moved on, pointing for the general store. Zurcher and Nemo would be in the saloon, directly opposite.

Pulling up at Gholson's, he dismounted, keeping the blue between the saloon and himself, and looped the reins around the bar. He paused then, probed the empty doorways and quiet shadows along the roadway, saw no one, but the hushed tension told him he was not alone, that the entire town was there watching — waiting.

He stepped from behind the blue, crossed to the saloon's porch in deliberate strides. Approaching the swinging doors from an angle, he stopped, peered into the dark interior. He could see the dim figure of the bartender, of a lone patron sitting at a table.

He let out a long breath, settled back on his heels. If Zurcher and the others were inside, they were back, out of his line of vision. Moving fast, he lunged through the batwings, whirled to face the hidden corner. There was no one there. Turning, he came back around, intending to question the bartender. His glance fell upon the lone customer. It was Morrel.

Anger whipped through Holloway. He crossed to the table. "Where is he?"

Dave raised his head. "If you're talking about Zurcher, I don't know."

"That's a little hard to believe."

Morrel shrugged, twirled his empty glass between his fingers. "Suit yourself. Fact is, I haven't seen him all day."

"Hard to believe that, too," Jess said in a low voice. "Next thing you'll be telling me you don't know he jumped the herd, shot up Tom Lindsey and some others, and slaughtered a lot of good beef."

Morrel was silent. He reached for the bottle before him, poured himself a drink. "No, I didn't know that. Tom bad hurt?"

"He'll live."

"Glad to hear it," Dave said, swallowing his liquor.

Jess smiled tightly. "I'll bet. Are you going to tell me where I can find Walt and Nemo?"

Morrel shook his head. "It's the truth. I don't know."

Holloway wheeled impatiently, threw his hard, pushing glance to the bartender.

The aproned man shrugged. "Ain't here. All I know."

Jess Holloway came fully around, strode to the doors, and stepped out onto the porch. He could have been wrong; Zurcher and his crowd may not have returned to town — could possibly have read the signs correctly and kept going. But that didn't sound like Walt Zurcher.

He had Dave Morrel tucked inside his pocket, had a good thing going — and with only one man standing between him and what he wanted, he'd not walk away now. No, Walt Zurcher would be around somewhere.

Jess eased off the porch and into the street, his eyes narrowed to shut down the sun's glare as he searched along the buildings. Near the center of the dusty roadway he came to a halt. Motion in the shadows just within the livery doorway caught his attention.

Imperceptibly he settled himself squarely on his feet. A faint coolness began to blow through him as his hand dropped to the pistol at his hip. A man emerged from the stable's entrance, started forward slowly. Holloway's muscles tensed. Nemo!

A second figure stepped into view, leaving the passageway just this side of the bakery. He was a tall, stooped man wearing two, low-slung weapons. He was one of those who had taken part in the raid; Holloway recognized the ragged Stetson he had pushed to the back of his head.

And then Zurcher.

Jess watched the outlaw walk into view from still a different point along the street, a fixed smile on his lips. They had set it up this way, placing him between them, he realized, thus making it impossible for him to face them all. Zurcher had stacked the odds.

Silent, he allowed them to approach. They were taking their time, hoping, perhaps, to shatter his nerve, force him to go for his gun without thinking and place himself in their cross-fire. He wouldn't play it that way. He'd wait — concentrate on Walt Zurcher; his death counted the most. If he still stood after that, he'd try to get off a shot at Nemo before he was cut down. He had no choice except to ignore the tall gunman, whoever he was.

Holloway heard a sound behind him, saw Zurcher and Nemo come to a stop. Dave Morrel's voice broke the warm hush that lay over the street.

"Reckon you could use some help."

Surprise rippled through Jess. Not removing his eyes from the three outlaws, he said: "You're standing on the wrong side."

"Not any more," Morrel replied, moving up to Holloway's shoulder. "I've done a lot of thinking. Guess I acted like a kid last night. Other times, too. But I grew up fast. Want me taking a hand in this?"

"Up to you."

Zurcher and the others had resumed their slow, indolent advance.

Jess said: "I don't understand this. You didn't know about that raid?"

"No. Something Walt cooked up on his own. I haven't seen him since yesterday when you tied us down on the buttes."

"I'm glad to hear that. The drive's going on through. Things'll be all right around here now. Lindsey's convinced."

"Same as me and Ma," Dave murmured, added: "Getting close enough. Who you want?"

It sounded like Saul Morrel speaking. Holloway grinned, said: "I can handle Zurcher and Nemo. You take care of the tall one."

"When?"

"Soon as they reach the front of the harness shop."

At that instant Nemo broke for his weapon. Jess drew fast, thumbed a shot at the man, whirled to face Zurcher. He heard Dave's gun blast twice as he turned, heard it again as he drove a bullet into Walt Zurcher and sent the outlaw staggering back, clawing at his chest.

He hung there, half bent, silent, as smoke coils floated around his head. And then, as tension broke and sweat began to glisten on his face, his taut shape relented. He turned to Morrel, saw him resting on one knee, clutching at a blood soaked spot on his thigh.

"That tall one . . . he was fast," Dave said with a wry grin. "But he was a mite low and wide."

Holloway dropped beside him, began to examine the injury. "Like your pa used to tell me, being fast was good. . . ."

"But being accurate was better," Dave finished. "Must've heard that a thousand times!"

Jess laughed, glanced down the street to the bodies of the outlaws. "We had us a good teacher," he said, getting up. He pointed to Morrel's leg. "Flesh wound. Not bad."

He turned, faced the people now rushing into the open. Several had gathered around the outlaws. Others were hurrying toward him and Dave. He beckoned to a couple of the nearest.

"Give him a hand to the doctor's," he said.

The two men crowded up, helped Dave to his feet. Morrel pulled away from them. "Where're you going?"

"Back to the valley. I've got that drive to finish."

"Hell, I can ride. I ought to be along."

Holloway shook his head. "Wait till next year. The way it looks now, I figure you'll be taking over right soon." Smiling, he crossed to the waiting roan.

ABOUT THE AUTHOR

Ray Hogan was an author who inspired a loyal following over the years since he published his first Western novel, *Ex-Marshal,* in 1956. Hogan was born in Willow Springs, Missouri, where his father was town marshal. At five the Hogan family moved to Albuquerque where they lived in the foothills of the Sandia and Manzano Mountains. His father was on the Albuquerque police force and, in later years, owned the Overland Hotel. It was while listening to his father and other old-timers tell tales from the past that Ray was inspired to recast these tales in fiction. From the beginning he did exhaustive research into the history and the people of the Old West, and the walls of his study were lined with various firearms, spurs, pictures, books, and memorabilia, about all of which he could talk in dramatic detail. "I've attempted to capture the courage and bravery of those men and women that lived out West and the dangers and problems they had to overcome," Hogan once remarked. If his lawmen protagonists seem sometimes larger than life, it is because they are men of integrity, heroes who through grit of character and common sense are able to overcome the obstacles they encounter despite often overwhelming odds. This same grit of character can also be found in Hogan's heroines, and in *The Vengeance of Fortuna West* (1983) Hogan wrote a gripping and totally believable account of a woman who takes up the badge and tracks the men who killed her lawman husband by ambush. No less intriguing in her way is Nellie Dupray, convicted of rustling in *The Glory Trail* (1978). One of his most popular books, dealing with an earlier period in the West with Kit Carson as its protagonist, is *Soldier in Buckskin* (Five Star Westerns, 1996). Above all, what is most impressive about Hogan's Western novels is the consistent quality with which each is crafted, the compelling depth of his characters, and his ability to juxtapose the complexities of human conflict into narratives always as intensely interesting as they are emotionally involving. *Land of Strangers* will be his next Five Star Western.

We hope you have enjoyed this Large Print book. Other Thorndike, Wheeler, Kennebec, and Chivers Press Large Print books are available at your library or directly from the publishers.

For information about current and upcoming titles, please call or write, without obligation, to:

Publisher
Thorndike Press
295 Kennedy Memorial Drive
Waterville, ME 04901
Tel. (800) 223-1244

or visit our Web site at:

http://gale.cengage.com/thorndike

OR

Chivers Large Print
published by AudioGO Ltd
St James House, The Square
Lower Bristol Road
Bath BA2 3SB
England
Tel. +44(0) 800 136919
email: info@audiogo.co.uk
www.audiogo.co.uk

All our Large Print titles are designed for easy reading, and all our books are made to last.